CAPTIVE

ANN VOSS PETERSON

CAPTIVE
Small Town Secrets: Sins, Book 2
Ann Voss Peterson

Welcome to Small Town Secrets

Three different series create the world of Small Town Secrets, and favorite characters like Val Ryker pop up in all of them. The stories can be read alone, as a series, or in chronological order.

Val Ryker Series- Thriller novels that feature police chief Valerie Ryker and firefighter David Lund.
    Small Town Secrets: Sins – Romantic thrillers that tell the saga of serial killer Ed Dryden and the brave men and women who finally stop him.
    Small Town Secrets: Scandals – Stand-alone romantic thrillers that take place in and around the small town of Lake Loyal, Wisconsin.

LETHAL (Small Town Secrets: Sins, Book 1)
    WITNESS (Small Town Secrets: Scandals, Book 1)
    MALICE (Small Town Secrets: Scandals, Book 2)
    STOLEN (Small Town Secrets: Scandals, Book 3)
    FORBIDDEN (Small Town Secrets: Scandals, Book 4)
    GUILTY (Small Town Secrets: Scandals, Book 5)
    KIDNAPPED (Small Town Secrets: Scandals, Book 6)
    PUSHED TOO FAR (Val Ryker Series, Book 1)
    BURNED TOO HOT (Val Ryker Series, Book 2)
    DEAD TOO SOON (Val Ryker Series, Book 3)
    WATCHED TOO LONG (Val Ryker Series, Book 4) *written with J.A. Konrath*
    CAPTIVE (Small Town Secrets: Sins, Book 2)
    FRANTIC (Small Town Secrets: Sins, Book 3)
    VICIOUS (Small Town Secrets: Sins, Book 4)
    BURIED TOO DEEP (Val Ryker Series, Book 5)

A DEVOTED TWIN

She grew up in foster homes, dreaming of having a real family. Then Sylvie Hayes met her twin sister. It should have been a joyous reunion, but when Diana disappears from her own wedding, and the cops believe Diana herself is to blame, Sylvie vows to rescue her twin... no matter the cost.

A SECRETIVE STRANGER

Attorney Bryce Walker has his own reasons for wanting to find the missing bride. Reasons that involve a notorious serial killer. When he offers to help Sylvie, he never expects to fall for her. But will she ever forgive his dark secret?

DARK PASTS COLLIDE

The closer they get to finding Diana, the closer they come to a shocking discovery that could destroy all they knew about the past... and all they hoped for the future.

A SISTER SEARCHING for her missing twin.
A lawyer seeking redemption.
A truth neither wanted to find.

CAPTIVE by Ann Voss Peterson
The past is a prison...

SMALL TOWN SECRETS: SINS

ANN VOSS PETERSON

-LETHAL
-CAPTIVE
-FRANTIC
-VICIOUS
Read them all!

Twenty years after LETHAL...

Sylvie

Sylvie Hayes dug her polished nails into the stems of her maid-of-honor nosegay and stared down the church's aisle. Faces peered expectantly from pews. Autumn chrysanthemums smothered the altar. The organ soared into Bach, rattling stained glass like thunder from an approaching storm.

It was her cue to start her measured march down the aisle. *But where was the bride?*

Sylvie glanced around the narthex for any sign of her twin sister. Diana had said she needed a moment to check her makeup, to make sure everything was perfect for her wedding. But that had been over fifteen minutes ago.

She should be back by now.

Sylvie and Diana might not know one another as well as twin sisters who'd grown up in the same household, but since Diana had tracked her down six months ago, they had become close. Closer than Sylvie had dared to get to another person.

Sylvie couldn't explain it. She'd always heard that twins were supposed to have a special connection, but she hadn't believed it until she and Diana had been reunited. Since, she swore she felt a sense of lightness when her sister was happy. And an insistent hum in the back of her mind when Diana was in trouble.

Right now, that hum threatened to drown out the organ.

Sylvie squinted at the shadows to the side of the altar. Although she spotted the minister talking to the best man, she couldn't see Bobby Vaughan anywhere either.

The groom was gone, too?

Sylvie turned away from the mouth of the nave and started for the lounge where she and Diana had dressed for the wedding. No doubt Diana was wrestling with her veil or her hair. Or maybe she and Bobby had argued.

At least Sylvie hoped it was something that simple.

Inside the lounge, makeup cases and dress bags cluttered the tables and draped to the floor. The spice of perfume still hung in the air.

But no Diana.

Sylvie opened the adjoining restroom door. The vanity was vacant, the wide mirror catching no reflection but her own. She peered down the row of bathroom stalls.

"Diana?" Sylvie's voice echoed off the white tile.

She gathered the seafoam satin of her gown in a fist. Bending low, she looked under the stalls.

A wisp of white touched the floor in the large stall at the end, a dark shadow behind it.

"Diana? Are you okay?"

Only the organ answered, its bass tones trembling through walls and centering deep in Sylvie's chest.

She raced down the row of bathroom stalls. Reaching the end, she knocked on the stall door. It moved under her fist. She grasped the handle and pulled.

A man lay prone on the floor, face against the wall. Wetness glistened in dark hair and trailed down the back of the tux. Motionless fingers clutched Diana's veil, the antique lace red with blood.

"Oh, my God, Bobby!" Sylvie knelt beside him. Slipping her hand along the side of his throat, she felt for a pulse.

A thready beat drummed against her fingertips.

He was alive. Thank God, he was alive. But he needed help. He needed an ambulance.

And Diana. Where was Diana?

The hum in Sylvie's ears roared loud as a freight train bearing down.

Diana

The hum of tires on pavement.

A gentle sway as the vehicle took a turn.

The light scent of blood, of carpet, of her favorite perfume.

Diana Gale tried to open her eyes, but her lids were heavy. So heavy. Her arm hurt... burned... She could tell it was dark... Must be late at night...

No. Something was over her eyes. Pressing down.

She tried to raise her hands, to touch her face, but she couldn't move.

What was going on?

Think...

Think...

She'd been at the church. She remembered that much. Getting ready for her wedding. About to walk down the aisle. To marry Bobby. It was perfect. The music. The flowers. Her dress. Just the way she'd always imagined. Happy. Relieved. Nervous. Then... nothing.

She didn't remember.

How could she not remember?

And then...

Then she was here.

Where was here?

The world swayed around her. She tried to breathe, to think, but she was tired, so tired. It blotted out everything.

She had to be dreaming.

Of course, that was it. She'd had nightmares the past few weeks. Mostly stupid things. Anxiety spinning and spinning through her mind, night after night. Walking down the aisle half dressed. Standing at the altar with no idea what to do, desperate for instructions, and Bobby laughing at her. The guests laughing at her. Her father laughing at her.

And now this.

She couldn't see. Couldn't move. Couldn't remember. And all she wanted to do was sleep. Just sleep.

This had to be a dream...

Sylvie

Paramedics wheeled the stretcher down the long church hall and out to the waiting ambulance. Bobby was still unconscious. The white sheet cupped around him as if he was a child tucked into bed. Thick black straps hugged him to the gurney.

Sylvie wrapped her arms around her middle, trying to warm herself, trying to feel strong. Stains marred the long seafoam silk of her gown, rust-colored smudges of Bobby's blood.

"You're the one who found him?" a cigarette-roughened voice asked from behind her.

She turned around and faced a man with hard eyes and the jowls of a bulldog. "Excuse me?"

He let out an impatient sigh. "I need you to answer some questions."

"And... who are you?"

"I'm in charge of this case. Detective Stan Perreth."

Sylvie dropped her gaze to the floor. She had never felt

comfortable around cops. Not since she'd been caught shoplifting a pack of chewing gum at twelve and the store manager requested she be "scared straight." It had taken her a long time to warm up to Bobby, and even now there were times she felt guilty of something just being around him.

"The first officer to the scene said you found Bobby Vaughan."

Sylvie forced a deep breath and made herself look the detective in the eye. "When I went to check on my sister."

"Did you touch anything? Move anything?"

"Um... I checked his pulse. I ran out into the lounge. I went through Diana's bag to find her cell phone." And she'd grabbed her own purse. Had she touched anything else? She couldn't remember.

He held out a hand. "Give me the phone."

Sylvie looked down. Sure enough, Diana's phone was still clenched in her fingers. She gave it to Perreth.

Perreth gripped it gingerly, his hands encased in clear plastic gloves. "Did your sister share her doubts about this wedding?"

"She's been looking forward to marrying Bobby as long as I've known her."

"Did she and Vaughan have a fight?"

Sylvie had wondered that same thing, but she wasn't about to tell the cop. "They were both excited about the wedding. Anxious to get married."

"Anxious." He scribbled the word in his notebook.

"You're taking this wrong. They were happy. They loved each other. They were eager to be together, to start their new life."

He nodded, but he didn't scratch out the word anxious.

Had Sylvie chosen that word subconsciously? Maybe.

Diana *had* been anxious the past few months. But not about Bobby. At least, not that Sylvie knew. "I don't think you're understanding me."

He glanced up at her from under bushy brows. "Oh?"

"Diana and Bobby were in love. They wanted to get married."

"Did you notice any tension between them recently?"

Back to the same track. "Between them? No."

"But you noticed tension."

"Diana seemed tense about something, yes. But not about her marriage."

He nodded, but she wasn't at all sure he had heard what she said. Not all of it, anyway.

"Where does your sister live?"

Sylvie gave him the address.

"Apartment number?"

"Three B."

He jotted it down. "Good, we'll get a warrant and take a look."

Unease niggled at the back of her neck. "If looking in Diana's apartment will help find her, I can let you in."

"Do you live with her?"

"I'm just visiting for the wedding." Sylvie had been considering moving to Madison and subletting her sister's apartment when Diana finished moving in with Bobby in Baraboo. Sylvie could just as easily wait tables in Wisconsin. But she hadn't yet taken the plunge. "Diana gave me a key, though."

"I need permission from someone with legal standing."

"Why?" The buzz in Sylvie's ears grew, making it hard to think. The only time she'd heard the term *legal standing* was on an episode of *Law & Order*. And then it had been used to argue the admissibility of evidence—evidence used against someone charged with murder. "You think Diana hurt Bobby?"

"I don't draw conclusions until I finish looking at the evidence."

"It sounds like you're drawing a conclusion to me. A wrong conclusion."

"I assure you that's not the case." He looked down at his notes. "But there was a history of abuse in your sister's adopted family, isn't that correct?"

"What are you getting at?"

"Adopted daughter showing up at school with bruises? Her mother, too. Walking into a doorknob? Falling down steps? Nice family, too. Plenty well off."

"If you have a point, you'd better get to it."

"They say women who are abused as children often choose men who—"

"Hold on right there. You think Bobby hurt Diana?"

The detective stared at her, a smug look in his deep-set eyes. "Like I said, I'm still looking at the evidence. But there's a good chance your sister was merely defending herself."

"Diana didn't do anything."

"A good attorney can probably get her off with a slap on the wrist."

"She didn't do anything."

"You need to tell her to turn herself in, though. It would make things a lot easier for her."

"What, have you already decided what happened without even looking at any of the facts? Some cop you are."

Bushy brows lowered over hard eyes.

Sylvie shouldn't have said that. And now that the words had left her lips, she couldn't bite them back.

Footsteps approached from down the hall. A uniformed officer stopped behind Perreth. "Detective?"

"Can it wait?"

"I think you're going to want to see this."

"Stick around. I'll want to talk to you further." Detective Perreth spun away and followed the officer.

Sylvie groaned. She shouldn't have insulted him, but she couldn't help it. He'd been right about Diana's adopted family, but that's where it ended. His accusation was ridiculous. How could he possibly think Bobby had abused Diana? That Diana had struck back? It would be laughable, even pitiful, if this Perreth character wasn't in charge of the case. If he wasn't the one who was *supposed* to be figuring out what really happened. The one who was *supposed* to be finding Diana.

Down the hall, Perreth followed the officer into the lounge. As soon as he rounded the corner, Sylvie started for the church's front door. She sure wasn't going to wait for Perreth to railroad her sister. She would find Diana herself, starting with taking a look in her apartment before Detective Perreth did.

Bryce

Bryce Walker had spent so much of the past week tracking down Diana Gale that when her apartment door opened and an ice-blue eye peered over the security chain, it took all he had to keep from kicking the door in, pinning her to the wall and demanding answers.

"Can I help you?" Her voice carried soft and low tones better suited to a seductress than a murderess.

Of course, there was no reason she couldn't be both.

"Bryce Walker. I'm an attorney. I need to ask you some

questions regarding a case I'm working on." His voice sounded as businesslike and detached as he'd hoped. As if this really was any case. As if he was merely doing his job for a client.

He reached into his pocket, pulled out a business card and slipped it through the narrow opening.

She accepted the card. "I don't think you want me."

"You are Diana Gale."

"Diana is my sister."

He peered through the small crack, trying to get a better look at her. Blond hair, large blue eyes, a heart-shaped face any man would enjoy seeing on the pillow beside him. A silver eyebrow ring pierced through the elegant arch of one brow, bringing a touch of rebellion to the picture. She held a hand to her chest, spreading pink-polished fingers across cleavage exposed by a formal green gown.

"I've seen your picture. And I know you're an only child."

"I'm Diana's twin. We were separated as toddlers."

She sounded sincere. But then, whatever she said in that musical voice would probably sound sincere. "What is your name?"

"Sylvie. Sylvie Hayes."

"And you live here?"

"I live in Chicago."

"Where in Chicago?"

"Why do you want to see Diana?"

Normally he might think her abrupt duck of his question evasive. But there was something in her voice. He wasn't sure what, but he got the distinct impression she was concerned. "Are you worried about Diana for some reason?"

"I want to know why you want to see her, that's all. So I can pass along the message."

A lie if he'd ever heard one. And in all the years he'd spent in the courtroom, he'd heard plenty. Not only was he sure she was worried, the prospect that she was telling the truth earlier seemed likely as well. Maybe she *was* Diana Gale's twin.

"I have a case to discuss with your sister." He peered over Sylvie Hayes's blond head, trying to see into the apartment through the small space in the door. "Will you tell her I'm here?"

"What kind of case?"

"The confidential kind."

"Well, Diana isn't home."

Was she telling the truth? Probably. "Where can I find her?"

"I'm afraid I don't know."

"When will she be back?"

"I don't know that either. But maybe if you tell me a little more about why you want to talk to her, I can help."

"If you don't know where she is or when she'll be back, I can't see how."

Her lips pressed into a thoughtful line. "You asked if I was worried about her?"

Maybe now they were getting somewhere. "Yes."

"I am. If you tell me what this is about, maybe I can make some sense out of things. For both of us."

Okay. He'd roll the dice. Since the client in this matter was actually himself, the case's confidentiality was as flexible as he needed. "I came across your sister's name yesterday. It was on the sign-in sheet at the Banesbridge prison. She visited an inmate there several times in the past year. I want to know why."

Pale blue eyes rounded in surprise. "Diana Gale?"

"Yes, Diana Gale."

Her eyebrows pinched together. "I don't understand."

"She signed in as part of a university research project under the supervision of a Vincent Bertram."

"Bertram?"

He did his best to tamp down his frustration. He wanted answers, not to listen to her parrot his every word. "He's a professor in the psychology department."

"Diana is earning her Ph.D. in English. I can't see her finding a lot of twelfth-century poetry in prison. Are you sure it was her?"

"The guards recognized her picture. The only other person it could have been is you."

"That doesn't make any sense."

"Of course, your sister might have used her affiliation at the university to gain access, and the visit was personal."

"Personal? How?"

"I was hoping you might have some idea."

"I'm sorry." Through the sliver of the opening, he could see her throat move under tender skin. "What prisoner was she visiting?"

He hesitated. The idea of saying the man's name to those delicate eyes already filled with fear felt cruel. And although his kid brother Tanner had accused Bryce of being heartless more than a few times when he'd hesitated to take his brother's charity cases, Bryce was not an abusive man. "My cell phone number is on that card. Have your sister call when she gets home. I'll be up late."

The door slammed shut followed by the rattle of the security chain. A second later the door flew open and Sylvie Hayes jolted into the hall. "Wait."

Bryce could tell she was attractive through the small space in the door, but he still wasn't prepared for the full view. The green dress flowed over smooth curves like water. Cheeks flushed pink under translucent skin. Wide eyes flashed with light-blue fire and more than a little desperation. "You have to tell me who she visited."

"It's confidential."

"I can probably pick up the phone and find out tomorrow."

"Then do that." At least *he* wouldn't be the one to break it to her.

"Who did she visit? Please."

Down the hall, a neighbor's door creaked open. A young man's spiked red hair poked out. Narrowing his eyes, he watched them with interest.

Bryce spared him a quick glance, then stepped toward Sylvie. "Invite me in."

"Tell me his name."

"Invite me in. We'll talk."

She backed into the apartment.

He followed her inside and closed the door behind him.

Sylvie stood her ground between the living room and a small dining area. "Okay. Tell me."

"As long as you tell me everything you know about your sister."

She nodded.

"Diana has been visiting Edward Dryden."

He'd thought it impossible for Sylvie's eyes to grow larger. He'd been wrong.

"The serial killer?"

"That's the one."

"No... Are you sure?"

"Your sister visited him once a month, starting seven months ago."

"That's a month before I met her." Her eyebrow ring dipped in a frown. "She never said anything about it. About him."

"You were worried about her. Before I came to the door tonight. Why?"

"She was supposed to be married today. But the wedding never took place."

That explained the fancy dress—a dress, he now realized, marred with brown smudges. "Is that blood?"

She nodded. "Right before the ceremony, I found Bobby—the groom—unconscious and bleeding. Diana was missing."

"You called the police?"

She curled her fingers to fists at her sides. "The police think *she* did it."

"Do you know for a fact that she didn't?"

She glared at the suggestion, as if considering leaving Bryce unconscious and bleeding if he didn't zip it. "The cop in charge made up his mind before he knew anything about what happened."

"Why would he do that?"

"I don't know. But he didn't care what I said. He'd already decided Diana was guilty, and I should convince her to turn herself in."

"So why aren't the police here? If they really suspect her, I would think they would be searching her apartment."

"I imagine they're on their way."

"And that's why you're here? To search her apartment before they arrive?"

She looked down. Her fingers tangled together. Busted.

"Then why are we standing around wasting time?" he asked.

She stared at him a long moment, as if trying to decide

whether she should trust him or not. Finally the press of time seemed to win out. "I thought I'd start in her office."

"Lead the way."

The office was a neat but obviously well-used workspace. White walls and desk gave the room a clean, fresh feeling. Papers rose in orderly stacked piles. But it was the splashes of color, the artwork and figurines dedicated to female superheroes, that made Bryce's lips twist in an ironic smile.

Too bad Diana herself was no champion of justice.

Sylvie sank into the desk chair, woke the desktop computer, and typed in the password. She clicked on various folders, scanning the files inside.

Bryce read over her shoulder. Student evaluations. Files dedicated to research. Drafts of her dissertation. Sylvie had searched through most of the document folder when Bryce noticed an unmarked, old-fashioned paper folder tucked behind the monitor. "What about that?"

Sylvie fished it out and flipped it open. A photo stared up at them—ice blue eyes in a face that looked much younger than its years.

The back of Bryce's neck prickled.

"This isn't..."

"Ed Dryden," Bryce supplied.

"He looks so normal."

Bryce couldn't argue. Some might even say he was good-looking. And that was exactly what made him so dangerous. God knew his civilized appearance had fooled Bryce at first. He tried to swallow the bitter taste in his mouth. "What else is in the folder?"

Sylvie turned the photo face down. Piled behind it were copies of newspaper articles, some more than twenty years old. The first few detailed Dryden's brutal murders of blond college coeds and his circus of a trial. Behind those were articles from '96 and '97 telling the story of his prison marriage to an eighteen-year-old girl named Nikki, his notorious escape, and his eventual recapture. More recent articles poked out from underneath in the original newsprint.

Bryce pointed to the photocopies on the top of the stack. "These look like they were made from microfilm."

"What's microfilm?"

"A way of storing outdated newsprint and magazines. Libraries used to use it in the old days."

"Why would she copy all these articles?"

"Don't know. Whatever the reason, she had to be pretty dedicated. It takes a lot of time to go through microfilm."

A piece of paper stuck out from behind the stack of articles: an envelope addressed to Diana Gale, complete with canceled stamp and postmarked last month.

Bryce's heart pounded so hard he could feel each beat in his throat. "Is that a letter?"

Sylvie let the copied article she was reading fall back into the folder and reached for the envelope.

A series of loud thumps sounded from the other room.

"Police," a muffled voice shouted from the hall. "Open the door. We have a warrant to search the premises."

Bryce met Sylvie's desperate eyes. They'd barely scratched the surface. He needed to study the folder, to find out exactly what Diana Gale saw fit to collect, what she knew about Dryden, and when she knew it. And most of all, he needed to read that letter. If it was from Dryden and he had sent it last month, it might give Bryce everything he needed.

Sylvie stuffed the letter back into the folder and snapped it shut. "I can't give them this."

"What are you planning to do?"

"I don't know. But I can't just hand it over. Detective Perreth will only use it to twist things, not to find Diana."

"You can't take it. That's removing evidence. It's a criminal action."

"It might be my only chance to find my sister."

And Bryce's only chance... No, he couldn't.

Could he?

Sylvie ran her hands over her gown. "I was going to change clothes. Why didn't I change clothes?"

There was no room in that dress to smuggle a folder, that was for damn sure.

Sylvie started for the door. "I'll throw it in my suitcase. I'll say I came to pack my clothes."

"If this detective has a brain in his head, he'll want to search your suitcase before he lets you walk out of here."

Bryce heard voices and the jangle of keys.

Sylvie looked around the room like a trapped animal. "What am I going to do?"

Bryce was an officer of the court. He couldn't interfere with a legal search warrant. He couldn't.

But could he give up the only lead he had?

"Oh, hell. Give it to me."

"What?"

It was crazy. Deluded. Definitely criminal.

Bryce watched his hand extend toward her, palm up, as if it was part of someone else's body. "Give me the folder."

Sylvie handed it to him.

He tossed his briefcase onto the desk, popped the locks and stuffed the folder inside. "Go ahead and pack your clothes. Quickly. I'll answer the door."

. . .

Sylvie

Sylvie jammed jeans, sweaters and toiletries into her suitcase. Her fingers were shaking so badly, she could barely grip the zipper and force it closed. In the other room she could hear the hum of voices. Perreth's blunt rasp followed by Bryce's level baritone.

When Bryce had hidden the folder in his briefcase, she'd been shocked. Sure, she'd asked for his help, for an answer to her dilemma, but she hadn't been expecting him to give her either. She certainly hadn't expected him to stick out his neck for her. No one had ever stuck their neck out for her.

So why had he done it?

Sylvie was sure he had his reasons, but she didn't have time to figure it out now. She finished closing the zipper and set the suitcase on its wheels. It was time to get out of here and get back to finding Diana.

Before it was too late.

Sylvie marched out of the office and down the hall. A small handful of police officers had already fanned out in the living room. Near the center of the room, Detective Perreth glowered at Bryce. Sylvie could smell his cologne of stale cigarettes.

"Nice to see you again, Ms. Hayes." He glanced at a uniformed officer who had begun sorting through the drawers in the coffee table. "Schmidt?"

"Detective?"

"Take a look through Ms. Hayes's suitcase, will you? We wouldn't want her removing anything other than her personal clothing from the suspect's apartment." He grinned, showing nicotine-yellowed teeth. "It's all right if he takes a look, isn't it?"

Giving him an equally phony smile, Sylvie left her suitcase at the mercy of the officer and reached out a hand to Perreth. "I want to see the warrant."

"I already showed it to your boyfriend here. And the super."

Bryce gave her a confirming nod.

"I asked you to stay at the church," the detective said. "Care to explain why that didn't happen?"

"I had things to do."

"Like what? Rushing to your sister's apartment to remove evidence?"

Hot pressure built in her head until it made her ears ring. This whole situation was so stupid. A judgmental cop throwing his weight around. And all the while, Diana was in danger. He should be *finding* her, not blaming her.

"I came back to change out of this dress and move my things to a hotel. That's all."

He eyed her gown. "What stopped you?"

"I did," Bryce said. "We had some things to discuss."

Things to discuss? Sylvie bit the inside of her cheek. Why would Bryce make a vague claim like that? Surely the detective would want to know more. Maybe enough to detain him for questioning. Or search his briefcase.

Next to her, the officer finished turning over her clothes and makeup.

"See, Detective?" she said. "Nothing. Can we go now?"

"Not so fast." Perreth focused his glare fully on Bryce. "What did you have to discuss that was so urgent?"

Bryce shrugged. "Doesn't that go without saying? Sylvie's sister disappeared."

"And what do you have in the briefcase?"

Bryce offered the detective a bland smile. "Papers."

"Maybe we should take a look at those papers."

"Sorry. Can't let you do that."

Perreth raised bushy brows. "Oh?"

"My briefcase is not listed in your warrant, for one thing."

"Maybe not. But if I suspect you of removing evidence from the scene…"

Bryce shook his head. "As an officer of the court, I can assure you that's not the case."

"You're a lawyer?" The detective pronounced the word as if it were composed of four letters.

Bryce gave him a cool nod. Turning to Sylvie, he cocked his head in the direction of the door.

Letting out the breath she was holding, Sylvie grabbed the handle of her suitcase and took a step toward escape.

"Not so fast," Perreth barked.

Sylvie's pulse pounded so hard it made her feel as if she was wobbling on her feet. Now what?

"Ms. Hayes still hasn't answered my questions. She's coming to the station with me."

The hum echoed through Sylvie's head, drowning out the beat of her pulse. She couldn't waste time sitting around the police station answering Perreth's pointless questions. Didn't they say that the first few hours were crucial to locating a missing person?

Bryce reached into the outside pocket of his briefcase and pulled out a business card. He held it out to Perreth. "Like I said. I'm a lawyer. Sylvie's lawyer. And my client will be happy to talk to you. If you give my office a call, we'll set something up."

Val

Valerie Ryker hadn't worked weekends since her days as

police chief of the tiny Lake Loyal police department. But when she ventured into the bar of The Lake Loyal Supper Club on this cool, fall evening, it wasn't to wait for a table to open up.

She spotted Harlan Runk bellied up, clutching his usual brandy old fashioned sweet. The man always looked as if he'd just wandered in from a multi-week hunting trip in the wilderness. Tousled gray hair. Ruddy skin. And eyebrows that resembled a bramble of wild blackberry. At least that hadn't changed.

His delight at seeing her hadn't changed either.

"Sweet buns! I missed you!" He kissed her on both cheeks, awkward, inappropriate, and somehow chivalrous all at the same time.

"I saw you at the grocery store just last week, Harlan."

"And it's been too long. You have to have dinner with me. Saturday is prime rib night, you know. Join me."

"I'd love to, but I'll have to take a rain check."

"Until after you've dumped that firefighter and admitted your undying love for me?"

Val chuckled, not sure what to say to that. "Lund sends you his best."

"I'll bet he does." Harlan raised his glass. "Buy you one of these?"

"I'm afraid I'm working."

"The sheriff's department now has its consultants pulling weekend overtime?"

"Not officially."

"But?"

"I was working on a case of Bobby Vaughan's."

Harlan rocked back a little on his stool. "How is Vaughan?"

"Stable but still unconscious."

"Poor bastard. Damn crazy shame to have something like that happen on his wedding day. I told him he should get married up here in Lake Loyal. Nothing like that happens up here."

Val wasn't so sure about that. She'd lived through some pretty insane stuff in Lake Loyal. And seeing that Harlan had been coroner of the county long before Val had moved to Wisconsin, she was sure he'd seen even more. In fact, one of those past times was the reason she needed a word with him now. "Listen, I know he was planning to go over something with you and—"

"You want my help finding out who attacked him?"

"I think the Madison police are handling that."

"Oh, yeah. Of course, they are. So what can I do ya for?"

"I was wondering if you could compare a couple of autopsies for me."

"Autopsies I performed?"

"Yes. Maybe I could stop by tomorrow or Monday morning, if—"

"Nonsense. I'll do it now."

"I hate to take you away from your dinner."

Harlan's bushy gray eyebrows pulled low. "Why would I need to leave my dinner?"

Val had seen him eat full meals in the morgue before, and it was an experience she'd rather not live through again. "Tomorrow or Monday would be fine. You can access your notes and—"

"Notes? I don't need notes. I can do it from memory."

"You don't even know what cases."

"I can guess. Try me."

"Uh, okay."

"The body that was found in the nature preserve five days ago and one Farrentina Hamilton, victim of Ed Dryden." He paused, as if letting the accuracy of his guess sink in.

Val nodded. "Those are the cases."

"Of course they are. And I'd love to talk to you about them all night, honey lips. So since you don't want to take me away from my prime rib, I guess you'll have to have dinner with me after all."

"Not in the morgue..."

"Of course not. Here."

Val gave in and let the hostess show them to a table. As a civilian, she couldn't do much in terms of actual law enforcement, not like the old days. She didn't have arrest powers and didn't carry a service weapon. Her official title was investigative consultant, but in fact her job wasn't a traditional job at all but a spot created specifically by a sheriff who was fond of her and said he didn't want the county to lose her expertise.

Expertise that was compromised by a body she could no longer trust.

Val pushed thoughts of her multiple sclerosis to the back of her mind. As long as her medication and health regimen kept her symptoms at a manageable level, she preferred to never think of the disease at all and focus on what work she was still able to do. So far, that philosophy had served her well. At least, when she stuck to it. The not dwelling on what she'd lost was the most difficult part.

After they'd ordered their prime rib specials, wolfed down a small appetizer of deep fried cheese curds, and returned from a trip to the salad bar, Harlan looked up from his "salad" of banana suspended in red Jell-O and asked, "So about those autopsies, what do you want to know?"

"You already answered that, in part," Val answered, picking at the beet pickles on her plate.

"I answered? How so?"

"You think the two bodies are related. Our new victim and a woman Ed Dryden killed twenty years ago."

Harlan's face broke into a wide grin. "Well, that was even easier than I expected. Case closed. You sure you don't want a cocktail? Maybe an old fashioned?"

Val held up a hand. Alcohol was one of those former pleasures she largely avoided now, along with hot showers and being a cop. "What I need to know is how."

"It's sort of a Wisconsin thing. Brandy old fashioned, sweet. You know, Wisconsin drinks more brandy than—"

"The bodies, Harlan. How did you know those were the two I would ask about?"

"Well, your current victim is the first homicide we've had in the county in a little while, so it only makes sense you would ask about her."

"But why Farrentina Hamilton? It's been twenty years, and her killer is in prison."

Harlan considered for a moment. "I think it would be easier to show you."

That was what Val had assumed from the beginning. "I can be at the morgue tomorrow morning."

"Oh, that's not necessary. I can show you tonight."

"After dinner?"

"Don't be silly." He smiled up at the waitress who was walking toward them with a full tray hoisted above her shoulder. "I can show you right now."

She set the steaming plates in front of them: rare prime rib swimming in au jus and topped with a dollop of horseradish, a baked potato ready to be split open, butter and sour cream on the side, and spears of tender asparagus kissed with, of course, more butter.

It smelled divine.

Val picked up her fork, ready to dig in.

Harlan held up a hand. "I'm that bastard Ed Dryden. I like thinking of women as animals. I also like thinking of myself as a hot-shot hunter. So I kidnap college girls, strip off their clothes, and let them loose in the forest. Then I take my hunting rifle and go after them."

Val glanced around the restaurant to make sure no one was picking up Harlan's rather odd and disturbing monologue. So far, so good. "Go on."

"Sometimes I shoot them, not to kill them, just hobble them. Sometimes I can catch them without wasting bullets. Sometimes I torture them just because it gets me off, sometimes I don't."

The couple at the closest table lowered their voices to whispers. Val could feel their fervent looks.

Harlan didn't seem to notice. "Either way, they all have ligature marks. And they all have scrapes and cuts on their bodies, since they're naked while they're running through the woods. And forest debris is sticking to the blood, particularly on their feet, knees, and palms."

"And both bodies shared all those characteristics."

Harlan beamed at her like she was his star student. "I'm waiting on analysis of the debris from that recent body, but from the look of it, it's from around here, just like it was with the Hamilton woman. Sand, pine needles, and the like."

"That doesn't seem like enough—"

"That's because we haven't gotten to the meat of it yet." Harlan picked up a steak knife. "The hunt is only part of what a hunter's gotta do. The next step is field dressing the carcass."

He brought the tip of the knife to the top of his slab of prime rib. "Ever see a hunter who really knows his stuff?"

Val shook her head.

"He, or she, is really fast with the knife. Decisive. They know just where to cut. First, they cut around the anus and free it, like coring an apple." Harlan slashed at the bottom of the roasted beef, slicing off a chunk of fat.

The couple next to them shifted in their chairs. Someone on the other side giggled nervously.

"Then he does a vertical cut, a little like the Y incision I use for autopsies." He sliced down the length of the meat, then spread it open with the blade. Blood oozed over the knife's serrated edge.

"Then he cuts through the diaphragm muscle and lastly the windpipe." He made a horizontal slash two thirds up the prime rib and another at the top. "And when all that's done, all he has to do is grab the trachea and pull, and all the organs come out with it."

Val was relieved Harlan had no way to demonstrate that little move. She glanced at the table next to them, seeing the same revulsion in the couple's expressions as she felt in the pit of her stomach. She mouthed the word *sorry* then returned her attention to Harlan. "So those steps were evident with both bodies?"

"Yes. But they didn't just use those steps. Both killers used exactly the same variations on those steps."

"I'm not following."

"Different hunters have different approaches to field dressing. Where they make their first cut, for example. Or how they free the anus. Or what they do with the entrails after. Some of 'em think of it as putting their stamp on the carcass, making it their own. But with Dryden, this was an even bigger deal."

Val suspected she knew where Harlan was going with this, but she wanted him to clarify anyway. "Bigger, how?"

"According to those *Silence of the Lambs* dudes, Dryden got off on the gutting more than all the rest. It was his art and his porn, if you know what I mean."

Unfortunately, she did. And judging from the horror on their neighbors' faces, they had an idea, too.

She tossed them another sorry, then homed in on the answer she needed most. "So it couldn't be an accident that the two bodies were this similar?"

"If one was found on the other side of the planet, I might consider it a coincidence. But in the same area of the same county as the last one?"

"And these details..." Val gestured to the mutilated prime rib. "They wouldn't have been in the media."

"Nope."

"So, it would have to be someone who knew all about Dryden."

"Yep."

She had another thought. A horrible thought. "And what says it wasn't the same person who killed both women?"

"For one, Dryden is in prison. For two, we know it wasn't someone else who killed Farrentina Hamilton, because there was a witness to her murder. For three, there's one more thing I haven't shown you." Harlan gestured to Val's prime rib. "May I?"

Not hungry in the least after this little show and tell, Val handed him her dinner plate. "Be my guest."

He plopped her slice of prime rib in front of him and

brandished the knife. "Remember how I cut my meat? Fast? With confidence?"

Val nodded.

"Well, that was the murderer twenty years ago, the one we know was Ed Dryden. And this? This is how our new mystery man accomplished his field dressing." Harlan started making the same cuts as before, only this time he moved his hand slowly, pausing, starting again. It took him three times as long, but he finally slid the mutilated meat in front of Val.

"See the difference?"

"You didn't know what you were doing, not like before."

"Right. And when you cut like that, you leave what we call hesitation marks. The recent murderer didn't have a lot of experience. He wasn't the master chef. He was just following the recipe."

"We're looking for a copycat," Val said.

Harlan nodded. "You're looking for a copycat."

SYLVIE

Safely outside Diana's building, Sylvie lowered herself into the plush passenger seat of Bryce's BMW. The scent of leather interior with a hint of cologne enveloped her, an atmosphere of luxury and male that made her feel as though she'd just stepped into a foreign world.

She'd rather walk.

Sylvie wasn't used to people taking care of her, doing her favors, making her indebted to them. She didn't like it. It reminded her too much of the way she'd felt as a child, begging her foster families to take her into their home, wanting so badly to be able to trust them to care about her, and being let down every time.

She strapped on her seatbelt and held her satin clutch in both hands. She didn't have a lot of options. Not with Diana's folder still locked in Bryce's briefcase. And although she was grateful to him for helping her smuggle the folder out of Diana's apartment, she didn't intend to take his kindness at face value. She'd learned that lesson before she hit puberty.

After loading her suitcase in the trunk, Bryce circled the car, opened the driver's door and slid behind the wheel. "Comfortable?"

She forced herself not to fidget. "How could I not be?"

"Car's for sale if you want it." He slipped his key into the ignition and the engine purred to life. Turning his attention to traffic, he shifted into gear and merged with the flow.

Sylvie eyed his profile in the dimming light. In all that had happened back at Diana's apartment, she hadn't been very aware of how attractive he was. From short golden-brown hair that held a slight wave to sharp hazel eyes to broad shoulders that looked good in a suit, Bryce Walker was what most women considered a hunk. Add ringless hands that gripped the steering wheel and he became a favorite for most eligible bachelor.

And somehow, that status only made Sylvie more uncomfortable. "Should I give you a retainer or something?"

He kept his focus on the traffic ahead. "Not necessary."

"What if Perreth finds out you're not really my lawyer?"

"Say you fired me."

"Why did you say it in the first place?"

One side of his lips kicked into a grin. "He was about to haul you downtown, if you hadn't noticed."

"Why would you care? You don't know me. And you sure don't owe me anything."

He turned his attention back to the road. "We have the same goal."

"Which is?"

"Finding your sister."

Ah, yes. His case. "Do you lie to the police and smuggle evidence to find witnesses in all your cases?"

"Not hardly."

"So what makes this different?"

A shadow crossed over his face. Evening had crept in while she'd been in Diana's apartment. But from Sylvie's angle, it looked more like a shadow of emotion rather than a simple trick of the light.

Bryce flicked on his blinker and took a left turn. "I'm not going to discuss my case, Sylvie."

"At least tell me what you want in return."

"You don't trust easily, do you?"

"And you don't answer questions."

"We both need to find your sister. Period."

"And that's it?"

"That's it."

Staring straight ahead through the windshield, she watched the glare of oncoming headlights. There was more he wasn't telling her. There had to be. Yet somehow that wasn't what concerned her most.

What concerned her most was that she couldn't afford to refuse his offer.

Bryce

Bryce pulled an extra chair up to the tiny desk in Sylvie's hotel room and set his briefcase on the laminate surface. For the first time, he had something tangible at his fingertips. Now, he was finally getting somewhere.

He lowered himself into the chair next to Sylvie. Her scent teased at him, flowers with some sort of spicy edge that made him want to inhale more deeply. The jeans and sweater she'd changed into did nothing to diminish her attractiveness. She might look like the photo he had of her sister, yet Sylvie had a freshness in the pink of her cheeks and the light sweep of her lashes that he'd never noticed in another woman. Even her pierced eyebrow suggested the spunky rebellion of a teenager. At the same time, she seemed so guarded and distrustful, he couldn't help but wonder why. He couldn't help but want to know more.

Shaking his head, he unlocked the briefcase. He couldn't afford to notice the way she smelled, the way she looked. He couldn't risk her becoming even a minor distraction. Forcing his attention where it belonged, he dropped the folder on the desk and flipped open the cover.

Ed Dryden stared at them from the five-by-seven photograph.

Sylvie flipped it face down. "I don't know how Diana could have stood being in the same room with him."

As someone who had been in Dryden's presence, Bryce couldn't help but wonder the same thing. But there were women who were drawn to serial killers. Why not Diana Gale? Dryden had certainly attracted more than his share of female fascination in the past.

Hell, years ago he'd convinced a woman to marry him in prison.

"No return address," Sylvie said, plucking the envelope from the pile of photocopies and clippings. She slipped the letter out and unfolded it. Reaching to the lamp, she canted the shade to shed more light.

The lamplight slanted toward Bryce and glared off the white paper, making it impossible to decipher the handwriting. But judging from the abrupt shape of the letters, it appeared to be written by a male hand. He waited for her to read it out loud.

"'You have no idea of the horror I've been through. My life is over. Ruined. And he will never pay. Not enough. So, you will pay for him.'" Sylvie looked up from the page, eyes stricken.

A din of questions swirled in Bryce's head. "Is it signed?"

"No. Do you think it's from Dryden?"

"Hard to say."

"Why would she keep it in this folder if it wasn't?"

"Why would Dryden threaten to make *Diana* pay? And who was she paying *for*?" He blew out a frustrated breath. "May I see it?"

Sylvie handed it to him.

It was just a single sheet of typing paper with the words she'd read scrawled across the white surface. He read it over again to himself. "He will never pay. Who is *he*?"

She lifted one shoulder in a shrug. "Who does Edward Dryden hate?"

"A lot of people." Including Bryce. He picked up the envelope and looked at the postmark again just to make sure. Almost exactly a month ago. *After* his brother Tanner's death.

"What is it?"

"Nothing." He handed the paper back to her. Was he wrong about Diana Gale? Was she another victim of Dryden's charm and brutality? Or had she merely outlived her usefulness? "Did your sister give any indication she was being threatened?"

Sylvie frowned, her eyebrow ring dipping low. "She's been worried the last several months. Anxious. I asked her about it, but she blamed it on problems with wedding plans. Do you think she reported this?"

"Maybe."

"Perreth didn't say anything."

"Maybe she didn't report it to the police."

"The university?"

"Maybe."

Sylvie pushed her chair back and shot to her feet. "What was the name of that professor? The one who arranged for her to visit Dryden?"

"Vincent Bertram."

She pulled out her phone and started a web search.

"What are you looking for?"

"A residential listing for Bertram. Maybe he knows why Diana got involved with Ed Dryden in the first place. And why he might have threatened her."

Bryce paged through the photocopies chronicling Dryden's sordid history. His murder of blond college coeds. His capture twenty years ago at the hands of the FBI. At that point, other than an article here and there, the news coverage skipped some years to a flurry of stories about Dryden's prison marriage and subsequent escape. The stories highlighted the way Dryden had focused on his new intended victim, Risa Madsen, a mentor of Vincent Bertram's. The stories continued with the trail of death Dryden had left until Professor Madsen and the FBI profiler who'd originally caught Dryden had joined forces to subdue him again.

"Maybe he is the FBI agent who caught Dryden."

Sylvie looked up from her phone. "Could be."

The next articles were more recent, clipped from their original newsprint. The headlines Bryce knew all too well. Headlines he'd *thought* he'd wanted. They blared from the clippings, stinging his eyes.

He'd been so stupid, so wrong, so naive. And he'd paid with more than his life.

He'd paid with his brother's.

Bryce sucked in a breath, trying to control the rush of grief, of rage, as he paged through the articles. The stories outlined Dryden's lawsuit against the Supermax prison, how attorney Bryce Walker had taken the killer's case, how he'd alleged mistreatment, how he'd won a transfer to another facility. Bryce flipped to the last article. A black-and-white picture stared from the newsprint, his brother Tanner in the black suit that made him look like an innocent milk-fed farm boy planning to hunt aliens with Tommy Lee Jones.

Bryce's throat closed.

He'd been willing to sell his soul to get good press for the law firm, for himself. He'd never guessed Tanner's life was part of the deal.

It seemed to Bryce that he'd paid enough. But maybe not to Dryden.

Bryce glanced up at Sylvie. She sat with her back to him, still scrolling through her phone. Hunching forward, she copied something on a scrap of paper.

What if her sister didn't have anything to do with Tanner's murder?

What if Diana was merely a misguided woman? A woman who never would have been able to worm her way into visiting Dryden if he was still housed in the ultra-security of the Supermax where he belonged?

What if Bryce's representation of Dryden had not only led to Tanner's death, but indirectly to Diana Gale's abduction as well?

Weight bore down on Bryce's shoulders like a yoke of stone. If he really wanted to set things right, maybe he shouldn't be asking himself if he could afford to help Sylvie Hayes. Maybe he should be asking if he could afford not to.

Diana

By the time the vehicle had stopped, Diana had been more coherent. By then, she'd figured out her wrists were bound in front of her with some kind of rope. Ankles too. A blindfold covered her eyes. And when large hands had hauled her into a building, deposited her on a bed, and secured her wrists to the frame, she'd been so afraid, she could barely breathe.

That had been hours ago.

Since, she'd just been lying here blind. Helpless. Whatever drug had incapacitated her at first had worn off, and there was no longer anything masking her terror.

This was no nightmare. Not in the dreaming sense. She'd been kidnapped.

Kidnapped.

Her mind still couldn't wrap around that.

She rubbed the back of her head against the mattress, slowly working the blindfold higher. Higher, until she could see a sliver of the room that was her prison. Cheap wood paneling covered the walls. Ruffled curtains framed a window in dingy white. The dimming light of evening filtered through dingy glass, leaving shadows hanging in corners. The room's door stood open, nothing but darkness visible beyond.

No, wait.

Something shifted in the doorway.

Someone was out there. Watching her.

She tried to suppress a shudder. "Hello?"

No answer.

But she was sure now—the movement, the soft sound of breathing—it wasn't her imagination.

"Please... you don't want to do this. Please, let me go."

She managed to move the blindfold a little higher. She could see the bed now and the white of her wedding gown. The bodice gaped open, delicate fabric torn from her neckline almost to her waist.

Diana had wanted to be sexy, for Bobby, for their wedding night. She never imagined some stranger would be staring at her instead, eyeing the pink of her nipples, well defined through the white lace bra.

She moved to cover herself, but her hands stopped short, the rope pulling against the steel bed frame.

"Oh, God, please. You've got to let me go. *Please.*" Diana hated the begging tone of her voice. The pleading note she'd had to use too often as a little girl.

It hadn't worked then either.

"My fiancé. He's a cop. He's going to be looking for me." As Diana said the words, a memory jiggled at the edge of her mind.

Bobby rushing to help.

Bobby hurt.

Bobby bleeding.

She tried to stifle a sob, but the sound eeked out in a strangled whimper. She had no one to protect her. No one to save her. And no clue how to save herself.

Tears clogged the back of her throat, but this time, she let them come. The pounding of her heart blotted out everything.

She was out of control.
She was helpless.
She was going to die.

Sylvie

With Professor Bertram's address stuffed in her jeans pocket, Sylvie crossed the hotel lobby with Bryce by her side and stepped through the revolving door and onto the sidewalk. Saturday night had fully fallen. The neon glow of nearby shops and restaurants, and the jangle of people walking down State Street turned the city into a confusion of sights and sounds.

Stepping to the curb, Sylvie glanced at the rush of headlights flowing down the one-way street. "Thanks for your help, Bryce. When I find Diana, I'll let her know you want to get in touch with her."

Bryce looked at her as if she were speaking in tongues. "I'm going with you."

"Not necessary."

"You need someone to drive."

"That's okay. I need to rent a car anyway."

"I have a car right here." He pointed to his car parked fifty feet away as if she'd forgotten what it looked like.

"Really, I'm used to doing things on my own." It had been disconcerting enough to be forced to rely on Bryce to get out of Diana's apartment with the folder. Having him in her hotel room, bouncing ideas off him, had only made her feel more jangled.

"How are you planning to find a car rental office? There aren't too many of them around here."

"I'll take a cab."

He arched his brows. "And how are you going to find a cab?"

What, was he playing games with her? "I'll hail one. It's not hard."

"You might find it a little harder in Madison."

She scanned the street. Not one cab spotted in the flood of personal vehicles. He might have a point. She pulled out her phone. "Okay, I'll Uber."

"What are you trying to prove, Sylvie? Driving you around is the least I can do. Besides, you need to find your sister, and I need to talk to her. We have shared goals here."

"Listen, it's not that I'm not grateful. But..."

"You don't like me?"

"I like you fine." Maybe too much. She doubted she'd ever been around a man this attractive before in her life.

"You don't trust me?"

"I don't want to be left in the lurch."

"Why would I do that?"

"Why wouldn't you?"

"Listen, you might have had bad luck with people in the past, but when I give my word, I keep it. No matter what." He gestured to the BMW. "Now are you going to get in, or do you want me to throw you in?"

"If you try, you'll get more than you bargained for."

He held up his hands, palms out. "Kidding. Listen, Sylvie, we made a deal. You help me with my case, I help you find your sister."

They had made a deal. A deal she wasn't comfortable with. Not in the least.

He glanced at his watch. "It's already pushing eight. Do you really want to stand around here and argue about this, or do you want to find your sister? It's up to you."

Diana had been missing for four hours. *Four hours* and the clock was ticking.

"Okay. For now."

Minutes later, Sylvie gripped the leather armrest and scanned the homes scrolling by, trying to spot the house numbers. When she'd first visited Diana in Madison, she remembered thinking the way the downtown funneled into an isthmus between two large lakes was charming. But after more than half an hour with Bryce negotiating hilly, winding one-way streets in the dark, the charm had worn off.

She finally spotted the address. A beautiful stone Tudor lit with artfully arranged spotlights and covered in ivy. "There it is."

Bryce piloted the car into the home's narrow drive, parked, and they walked up the cobblestone sidewalk. Bryce stabbed the doorbell button.

Chimes echoed through the house. A moment later footsteps tapped across a wood floor inside and an eye peered through the peephole.

"Yes?" A woman's voice.

"My name is Sylvie Hayes and this is Bryce Walker." Sylvie projected her voice, hoping the woman could hear her through the door. "We'd like a word with Professor Bertram. Is he home?"

"No."

"Do you know when he will be home?" Bryce asked.

"No."

"Is this Mrs. Bertram?"

Silence.

Strange. Wisconsin Heights was not a neighborhood that seemed to call for a lot of security. Mostly home to university professors and well-to-do business leaders in Madison, it seemed like a safe neighborhood in an area overflowing with safe neighborhoods. Except for the nighttime visit, which would make anyone wary, there didn't seem to be a reason for Mrs. Bertram's apparent fear.

Sylvie couldn't help but wonder what or who had spooked her.

Bryce raised his eyebrows at Sylvie. "We need to talk to Professor Bertram about a graduate student who is working with him on one of his research projects."

"My sister, Diana Gale," Sylvie added.

"He doesn't live here anymore. He hasn't for many years."

"You're divorced?"

"That's what I'm saying."

Disappointment seeped into Sylvie's bones like the chill of approaching winter. "Do you have his address?"

"Of course I have it. That doesn't mean I'm going to give it to you."

"We really need to talk to him. My sister has disappeared."

"And you think Vincent can help you?"

"We hope so," Bryce answered.

"What project was your sister working on for Vincent?"

Sylvie hesitated. "Diana interviewed Ed Dryden."

She could hear Mrs. Bertram's sharp intake of breath even through the door. Silence followed that was so complete Sylvie thought the woman might have walked away.

Suddenly the clack of two deadbolts sliding open cut the quiet. The door inched open and Mrs. Bertram peered out. Skin nearly as white as her hair, she blinked even in the darkness, like a mouse venturing out of a safe, dark hole. "Stop by Vincent's office. He'll be happy to help all he can."

"I was really hoping to talk to him before Monday," Sylvie said.

The woman glanced at her watch. "He's probably there now."

"On a Saturday night?"

"He usually stops back after dinner, says it's quieter then, better for concentrating. But if your sister's disappearance has something to do with that monster, he won't mind the interruption. He'll do everything he can to help."

Sylvie wished she could shake the woman's hand, something to let her know her appreciation. But Sylvie got the feeling that a touch from a stranger wouldn't be welcomed. She settled on a smile. "Thank you so much."

The woman gave her a nod and retreated, closing the door behind her.

Sylvie glanced up at Bryce, eager to get his impression of what had happened.

He was looking past her, in the direction of the street.

She followed his line of sight. The one-way street was quiet. Except for an older man walking a dog and a blue service van pulling into a side street, it looked as though the entire neighborhood was spending Saturday night either out or snuggled in their living rooms. "What do you see?"

"I'll tell you in the car."

Sylvie had just enough time to climb in the BMW and secure her seatbelt before Bryce pulled away from the curb. "Okay, out with it."

Eyes flitting to the rearview mirror, he slowly wound through the quiet neighborhood. "Did you notice the van?"

"Are you thinking it's strange for a service van to be driving around on a Saturday night?"

"Yes, but that's not all."

"I hate playing guessing games. Will you just tell me?"

"It belongs to a food service. The type of business that provides produce, meat and canned goods to institutional settings like nursing homes."

That was about as straightforward as another riddle. "Okay, I'll bite. You're wondering what a food service van was doing in that neighborhood?"

He nodded. "On a Saturday night."

Okay, so that did seem odd. But there could be a perfectly innocent explanation. "Maybe a higher up in the company lives there."

"Did you see the driver?"

"No."

"Remember the redheaded guy who was listening in on our conversation in the hallway of your sister's building? Diana's neighbor?"

She hadn't paid much attention to him, not enough to pick him out in a crowd. "He's driving the van?"

"It's dark, but yeah, I'm pretty sure it's him."

Sylvie twisted sideways in her seat as if she was talking to Bryce. Covertly she glanced out the back window. Sure enough. Several car lengths back, she saw the hulking shape of a panel van. "Why on earth would Diana's neighbor be following us?"

Bryce veered right. "I don't know. But I aim to find out."

Bryce

Bryce let up on the gas and watched the distance between them and the van shrink. He didn't want to lose Red. Not yet.

"What are you going to do?" One hand clutching the armrest and the other bracing against the padded dash, Sylvie looked as if she expected him to take off cross country, four wheeling it through manicured yards and flower gardens.

There was a day when he might have been arrogant enough to try something like that, just for fun. But *that* Bryce had died along with Tanner. "I'm going to set a trap."

He drove several blocks before the narrow road branched off to the left. He flipped on his blinker, making sure their red-haired shadow got a good look before he turned.

"What kind of trap?"

Bryce drove slowly down a road flanked by forest-shrouded homes. "This drive loops in a circle. Once our guy follows us in, there will be no way for him to drive out without going past us."

No need to explain how he knew this, how he used to pass the little jog in the road sheltered by trees every day on the way to the office—the place he now planned to lie in ambush. Driving through this neighborhood was reminder enough of things he wished he could forget.

The road split into two branches, one gliding straight up a hill, one turning sharply into a copse of trees. Bryce chose the hill.

Sylvie twisted in her seat. "He's turning in behind us."

"So far, so good." He kept his speed steady, climbing the hill and driving along the crest. He glanced in the rearview mirror. The panel van was hanging back, waiting until they crested the hill before following. Red didn't want to be seen.

Too late for that.

"What are you going to do once you trap him?"

"Ask him why he's following us."

Up ahead a real estate sign attracted his attention. The

windows in the mansion behind it were black and as empty as soulless eyes.

Bryce focused on the road ahead and kept driving. He'd drop the price again if it didn't sell after the open house tomorrow. Hell, he'd give the sucker away. Anything to be rid of it. To be rid of the man he once was. And then he'd junk his boat and this car for good measure.

They crested the hill and curved down the other side. Reaching the sharp turn near the creek, he pulled to a stop in the cover of trees. From here they could see both branches of the loop. And anyone following couldn't see the BMW until they were nearly on Bryce's bumper.

Bryce unhitched his seatbelt. "Stay here."

"What if he has a gun?"

"I'm just going to talk to him."

"And that's going to keep him from shooting you?"

"Why would he have a gun?"

"I don't know. It seems like everyone has a gun anymore."

Bryce had to admit, it hadn't occurred to him that Red could be armed, and now that it had, he wished he had a pistol of his own about now.

Too late for that. "Stay here," he repeated, and climbed out. He heard the passenger door open before he rounded the back of the car.

Why did he ever think Sylvie would listen to him?

The sound of an engine coasted down the hill and wound toward him. Rounding the corner, the van emerged from the trees. Brakes locked up, rubber screeching against pavement. The driver stared through a bug-spattered windshield, his skin pale even for a redhead. He threw the van into reverse and hit the gas. The engine roared. The van shot backward and slammed into the trunk of a tree.

The sound of steel crumpling made Bryce wince. He'd meant to make an impression, not cause an accident. But the damn kid got what he deserved. Catching up to the van, Bryce yanked open the door.

Red held up his hands as if Bryce were pointing a gun at him after all. "I didn't do anything. I swear."

At least Red seemed all right. "Why are you following us?"

"Following you? I'm not following you."

"And you expect me to believe that?"

Out of the corner of his eye, Red spotted Sylvie step alongside the panel van's snubbed hood. She narrowed her eyes on him. "Who are you?"

"Louis...Louis Ingersoll." He latched on to Sylvie with his gaze. "You're Diana's twin sister. She told me about you."

"What do you know about Diana? Where is she?"

"Diana? That's why I was following you. I hoped you'd know."

Right. As if Bryce believed that one. "Why didn't you just ask?"

"I was going to."

"Come on out of the van and talk to us for a minute."

The kid looked from Sylvie to Bryce and back again. "I don't know anything about what happened to Diana. I just know what the minister told everyone in the church. I swear."

Sylvie stepped toward him. "You were at Diana's wedding?"

"Of course. She's my neighbor. I might not have agreed with her marrying that Baraboo cop, but it doesn't mean I'm not going to show for the wedding if she wants me there."

"You weren't a big fan of Diana getting married?" Sylvie asked.

"She was too good for him."

"Why do you say that?" Sylvie asked. "What do you know about Bobby?"

"Nothing. Just that he's a cop."

Bryce remembered Detective Perreth's suspicions where Bobby was concerned. Suspicions Sylvie had written off as ridiculous but might be worth checking out. "Did Bobby and Diana fight often?"

Even though Bryce kept his focus on Red, he could feel Sylvie's glare burn a hole just in front of his ear.

Red slid out of the van. Hitting the ground, he shifted one of his Reebok runners in the gravel. "You're thinking the same thing that detective at her apartment was thinking. That he beat her up."

"Did he?"

"If he had, I would have killed him." He balled his hands into fists.

Bryce didn't know Bobby Vaughan, but he would have to be pretty small to be overpowered by Red. Posturing aside, Red still hadn't answered his original question. "Did they fight often?"

Red's hands went slack by his side. "I never even heard them argue."

"Did you tell that to the detective?" Sylvie asked in a righteous tone, shooting Bryce a glare.

"He didn't seem to care."

So maybe Sylvie was right about her sister and Bobby Vaughan. Maybe. Bryce had to admit that whatever the truth was, the longer he was around Sylvie, the more he wanted to believe her version. "So why do you think Diana is too good for her fiancé?"

"Do you know her, man? Have you ever met her?"

"No."

"She isn't just beautiful, she's smart. You know, like lightning smart." He stared dreamily, as if picturing Diana in front of him now. Only he was staring at Sylvie. "And she has this smile that seems like it's only for you."

Bryce hadn't had much chance to experience Sylvie's smile, but he could imagine what it felt like way too vividly.

He pulled himself back from that thought. "So you have some kind of puppy-dog crush on Diana?"

Red lifted his chin, defensive. "She was my neighbor. And my friend."

Now he'd made the guy defiant. A great way to get him to open up. He needed to keep his head straight, remember what he was trying to do, not go off on mental tangents like pondering Sylvie's smile.

Next to him, Sylvie focused on Red, nodding understandingly. "It sounds like you would know everything that went on in her life."

"Not everything."

"Maybe enough to help us find her? To help us save her?"

The kid drew himself up. Like any red-blooded guy with a crush, he liked the idea of being a knight in shining armor to Diana Gale's damsel in distress. "How can I help? What do you need to know?"

With just a few words, Sylvie had tapped into Louis Ingersoll's vulnerabilities immediately. Bryce stood back and watched, letting her take over.

"You said Bobby wasn't good enough for her. Why?"

"He was there in the room where she disappeared, right? And he didn't protect her. I would have protected her."

"How did you know Bobby was there?"

"The detective. He told me."

Perreth hadn't been overly eager to share information

with them. Why would he have confided that detail to Diana's next-door neighbor? A next-door neighbor nursing a serious crush?

The uneasy feeling resumed its creep up Bryce's spine. Thanks to Tanner's penchant for helping abused and vulnerable women, Bryce had seen more than his share of injured male pride and thwarted male desire. This kid had it bad for Diana. And Diana was to marry another man. All the elements for disaster. "You could have done a lot of things for Diana Gale, couldn't you?"

The kid stuck out a freckled chin. "Yeah."

"But she wouldn't let you."

The chin hardened. "Hey, it's not my fault if she was fooled by that whole man-in-a-uniform thing."

"You think Bobby fooled her? You think that's why she wasn't interested in you?"

"Diana and me... we were close. We talked all the time. I knew things she didn't tell anybody else. Not even that cop."

"Like what?"

"You think I'd repeat them to you?"

Sylvie stepped forward and laid her hand on his arm. "Will you tell me? Will you help me find my sister?"

Bryce watched the kid's defiance fall apart like a bad court case. First the chin receded. Then his eyes softened to the consistency of that sweet creme inside fancy chocolates.

"Did Diana ever mention the name Ed Dryden to you?" Sylvie asked.

"Sure. I used to save clippings for her from the newspaper. She was fascinated with him."

"Did she say why?"

"She didn't need to explain. We have always been on the same wavelength."

"Can you explain it to me?"

"Ed Dryden is..." He shrugged. "A lot of people find serial killers interesting."

Sylvie shook her head as if she couldn't understand the comment and refused to accept it would include her sister. "Do you think he has anything to do with her disappearance?"

"He's in prison."

"Do you know why he would want to hurt Diana?"

"Why do you think he wants to hurt Diana?" Shaking his head, Red offered Sylvie a reassuring smile. "No one would want to hurt her. Everyone loves Diana."

The unease encircling Bryce's throat gave a squeeze. Maybe everyone didn't love Diana, but this kid sure did. To the point of obsession. And judging by the way he was looking at Sylvie, after this little chat his obsession might just include her too.

Sylvie

Fortunately, parking on the university campus was easy to come by on a Saturday night. But amidst the university-wide construction, finding the psych building was another matter. As uneasy as Sylvie felt about Bryce accompanying her, she couldn't help but be grateful; at least he knew Madison. Had she been trying to negotiate the campus alone, she probably would have been walking aimlessly all night. Instead, Bryce led her through the maze of buildings with confidence, finally locating the temporary offices serving the psychology department while it appeared the psychology building itself was being torn down and rebuilt.

It was so quiet in the building, she was surprised to find

the door unlocked. A glance at the directory inside the door told them which professors' offices were being housed here and how to find them.

"No Risa Madsen. She must not be at the university anymore."

Bryce tapped the glass covering the directory board. "But Vincent Bertram is here."

They climbed the stairs to the second floor and wound through a narrow hall until they found his office.

Bryce knocked on the door.

No answer.

"We must have missed him." They couldn't wait until tomorrow. Since Diana had disappeared this afternoon, alarm had been blaring in Sylvie's ears nonstop. She had to find her sister *now*.

"Are you looking for someone?"

Sylvie whirled toward the quiet voice.

A man only a few inches taller than she, but with the wide shoulders of a bodybuilder, strode down the long hall toward them. His blond hair was liberally sprinkled with white and tapered into almost fully white sideburns that matched his goatee. But the most striking thing about the man was his brown eyes. The dark irises were almost completely surrounded by white, making his gaze very intense. "Diana?"

She fought the urge to squirm. "I'm her sister, Sylvie."

"Oh, forgive me. I didn't know Diana had a twin." He stuck out his hand. "Vincent Bertram."

Sylvie barely contained a relieved sigh. "I need your help. It's about Diana."

His palm engulfed hers, enveloping her hand in a sort of fatherly warmth that contradicted the intensity of his eyes. "Of course. Come in."

Professor Bertram slipped a key into the lock and gestured Sylvie and Bryce into a small, book-lined room barely bigger than Diana's walk-in closet. The only thing that kept the room from inspiring claustrophobia was the single small window overlooking the lights dotting Bascom Hill. Thankfully he left the door open.

"I'm sorry for the cramped office. These are our construction digs. They tell me the new psychology building will be beautiful."

Sylvie returned his smile and nodded at the window. "Your view is beautiful."

"That, I'm afraid, won't be quite so nice in the new building. Have a seat, would you?"

Sylvie and Bryce lowered themselves into chairs.

The professor leaned a hip on the edge of his desk and peered down at them. "Now, what can I help you with?"

Sylvie again found herself fighting the need to squirm. She'd hate to have Bertram as a professor. Sitting under those eyes made her feel as if he could see right through her. "I need to know why my sister is involved in your research."

"The research on Ed Dryden, yes." Seemingly Professor Bertram had no qualms about saying the killer's name out loud. But then, that kind of comfort probably came with poring over what the man did and said on a regular basis. One grew desensitized.

Sylvie thought of the photo of Dryden and all the articles describing what he'd done. Had Diana become desensitized to Dryden's evil too? Did the horror of what he was simply wear off over time?

Sylvie couldn't imagine it.

"Our arrangement is very simple, actually. Diana asked to help, and I took her up on it."

Bryce gave an incredulous grunt. "And you let anyone who asks waltz into a maximum-security prison and chat with a dangerous serial killer?"

"Of course not. Diana was different."

"How?"

"I've done a lot of work studying serial killers, put in a lot of years. Studying Ed Dryden was going to be the crowning jewel of my career. I even talked to a publisher for my book on the subject. Then Dryden decided to be difficult."

Bryce leaned forward in his chair. "Difficult? How?"

"He refused to let me interview him further."

"So your book deal was dead." The picture was coming clearer in Sylvie's mind.

"More than that. All the research Risa Madsen had started and I had continued on Dryden came to a dead end." He shook his head.

"Enter Diana?" Sylvie said.

"Somehow she'd found out about our work. She asked if she could be part of the program."

"That still doesn't explain why you let her." Bryce's tone was unmistakably condemning. But though Sylvie found the hints of protectiveness he'd shown her nerve racking, she warmed to the idea that he might feel protective of Diana as well.

"Diana said she was going to speak to Dryden whether I arranged it or not. So I arranged it. Why wouldn't I? There was no program without her. No book. Not one of much merit, at any rate. Dryden wasn't going to let me interview him. But here comes this intelligent woman who wants to give my work a chance at a second life. And Dryden agreed to speak with her."

Sylvie couldn't believe it was that simple. "Didn't it occur to you that you might be putting her in danger?"

"Banesbridge might not be as restrictive as the Supermax, or whatever it's currently called, but it's being totally renovated. It's secure."

"It would probably be more secure if Dryden wasn't allowed to communicate with anyone who wanted a chat."

Bertram met Bryce's comment with a bland look.

Sylvie shot Bryce a warning glance. Shifting in her chair, she returned her focus to Bertram. "Did Diana report a threatening letter she received from Dryden?"

"A letter?" He seemed genuinely surprised. "When?"

"About a month ago," Bryce informed him.

"She didn't mention it." Graying brows hunkered low. "Why don't you ask Diana these questions?"

"Diana has disappeared."

"Disappeared? How?" He raked a hand through his hair, fingers trembling slightly. "Is that why you're here? You think Ed Dryden somehow *caused* her disappearance?"

She wanted to say yes, but the answer seemed ludicrous. Ed Dryden was an evil man, but he wasn't some sort of supernatural being. He couldn't attack Bobby and kidnap Diana from his prison cell. "To tell you the truth, Professor, I came to talk to you because I don't know what to think."

"Have you reported this to the police?"

"Yes."

"Have they found anything?"

"The detective on the case isn't very forthcoming. I don't know what he's found."

The professor raked his hair again. "I'm sorry. Is there any reason you believe Edward Dryden might be involved?"

"Just the threat she received."

"The threat?" He shook his head. "She never told me he threatened her."

"We're not sure it was him."

"Who else could it be? And why wouldn't she have told me?"

"Maybe because she knew you wouldn't allow her to see him anymore?" Bryce offered.

"I wouldn't have. I want you to know that. If I thought she was in any danger at all, I wouldn't have let her near him." He looked to Sylvie. "I'm so sorry, Sylvie. You can't know how sorry I am that any of this had to happen."

She pushed herself up from her chair. "Thank you."

He grasped her hand in his. "The police know their job. I'm sure they'll find her."

At least someone was sure. "If you think of anything at all, will you call me?"

Grabbing a pen from the desk, Sylvie jotted down her cell number. Bryce handed him a business card before following her out of the office.

They walked a short distance down the hall without saying a word. For a reason Sylvie couldn't name, she wanted to get out of Professor Bertram's earshot before chewing over all he'd told them—and more importantly, all he hadn't.

Rounding the corner, they nearly ran headlong into a dark-skinned man wearing glasses with the largest lenses Sylvie had ever seen. Behind the glasses, the lines of middle age crinkled around sharp black eyes. "Don't believe Bertram's innocent act."

"What?" Sylvie couldn't have heard him correctly, could she? "Who are you?"

"Sami Yamal. Assistant professor. I couldn't help but overhear. You want to know more? Come." He motioned for them to follow and walked off down the hall.

Once they passed the stairs and rounded another corner, Yamal unlocked an office and led them inside. Cubicles and file cabinets jammed a room three times the size of Bertram's office. As soon as they stepped inside, he closed the door behind them. "Your sister was obsessed with Ed Dryden."

Sylvie thought of the file folder Diana kept on the serial killer. As much as she wanted to argue against his charge, she couldn't. "Why do you think that?"

"Things she said. Things she knew."

"Like what?"

He waved a hand, as if brushing the details away like stray crumbs. "Let's just say she did her research before she ever set foot in this department. And that was just the beginning. She wouldn't let it go. She grilled me."

"Why would she grill *you*?" Bryce asked. "Why not go directly to the expert?"

"Expert? You mean Bertram?" He raised his chin, clearly prickly over Bryce's question. "I might not have tenure like Bertram, but *I* was the one who kept the Ed Dryden research going in the years after Risa Madsen left. Diana *did* come to the expert."

"And what did you tell her?"

"I answered her questions."

"And suggested she talk to Dryden herself?"

Yamal held up a hand. "I told her not to go near him. Bertram pushed that."

"Bertram?" Sylvie glanced back in the direction of Bertram's office. Had he lied to them? Why? "He said Diana insisted she would visit Dryden whether he arranged it or not."

"Diana was eager to know about Dryden, no question. But that was it. She never asked to visit him. Until Bertram decided she was the savior of his book deal."

Bryce arched his brows. "So you're saying Bertram pushed her into visiting Dryden?"

"Bertram used Diana. And she was happy to let him."

Sylvie nodded. That much Bertram had told them, if not in so many words. "He implied Dryden agreed to talk to her because she's a woman."

Yamal let out a short, barking laugh. "Not just any woman."

"What do you mean?"

"Have you ever seen pictures of the women Dryden killed?"

The faces from the news articles Diana collected filtered through Sylvie's mind. "Some of them."

Yamal's smile made her want to squirm. He opened a file drawer and pulled out a folder. Carrying it to a nearby desk, he removed a stack of photos. "One look at these and you'll understand."

A nervous flutter lodged under Sylvie's ribs.

Bryce stepped up beside her. He placed his hand lightly on her arm, as if to offer support.

She pulled her arm away. She could make it on her own. Whatever Sami Yamal was about to show her, she'd deal with it as long as it led her closer to finding Diana.

One by one, Yamal spread a variety of shots of smiling blond women across the desktop. "These are Dryden's first victims, the ones he killed before he was captured the first time. Notice the similarities? They're all young. They're all blond."

Sylvie didn't have to look hard to see what he was talking about. "And they all look like Diana."

He pulled one of the pictures from the rest and held it in front of Sylvie's nose.

She nearly gasped. The woman in the picture could be her third sister—not identical, but frighteningly close. The style of the woman's blond hair and the puffy sleeves of her jacket dated the picture. No doubt the woman would be quite a bit older than them—if she had lived. "Is that his first victim?"

He shook his head. "His last. Well, until his later prison escape. But she is the most significant of his early victims."

Bryce nodded. "His wife."

"Adrianna Dryden. The theory first developed by Risa Madsen is that Dryden had felt controlled by her, a control he couldn't fight against, a control that emasculated him. So he killed women who looked like her to claim back the power he felt she stole." He gestured to the collection of photos with a sweep of his hand. "In effect, he used these other murders to fantasize about torturing, murdering, and mutilating his wife. When he finally worked up enough confidence and excitement, he did what he'd aimed to do all along."

Sylvie swallowed into a dry throat. "And Diana looks just like her."

"Exactly why Bertram knew Dryden would talk to her. And Diana wasn't interested in taking credit for the research or the book. A match made in heaven." Bitterness turned his voice as brittle as a crust of ice. "Diana Gale never should have been put in that situation. She didn't know Dryden. She might have hit the microfilm, but she didn't do the years of research required to learn how to handle someone like him, if it's even possible. I don't know if Ed Dryden is responsible or not for your sister's disappearance, but if he is, the blame lies squarely with Vincent Bertram."

Val

Val smelled the body before she saw it. The sweet, putrid odor of decay threaded through scents of autumn leaves, nighttime, and lake. She signed in with the officer maintaining the crime scene record, ducked under the yellow tape, and followed the lights illuminating the forest path.

"Glad you could make it down here so fast," a bulldog of a man said. He motioned her to follow. "Coroner wants to cut her down asap. Rain coming."

"Detective Perreth, I presume," Val said to the Madison cop.

"Sorry. Call me Stan. I recognized you from your picture. You know, a few years ago."

For a while there, Val's face was all over the media, local and even nationwide. A statement like Stan's was usually followed by a battery of questions about Dixon Hess and the hell that had unfolded in Lake Loyal. She wasn't eager to walk down memory lane. "Tell me about what you found."

"I've done some deer hunting in my day, and what he did to her..." Stan paused, as if gathering his composure. "It's messed up."

Val nodded. Murder was messed up. And an investigation was always emotionally stressful. As long as she kept it compartmentalized, as if this murder were more a mind puzzle than a horrible tragedy, she could function. Later, after her job was done, she would tackle the job of processing. Now her focus had to be on finding whoever was committing these horrible crimes and helping law enforcement stop him.

"So are you saying she was field dressed, the way a deer would be?" she asked Stan Perreth.

"That's why I called you. I was a rookie at your county sheriff's department back when Ed Dryden went on his last spree. This seems a bit too familiar for comfort. And then I heard you have another one, a recent one…"

"You heard right."

"Copycat?"

"Seems likely. Maybe our county coroner could consult with your M.E?"

"Sure thing. Appreciate it."

They kept following the trail, the smell growing stronger with each step.

"Was there anything else you noticed?" Val asked.

"He went to certain lengths to hide the victim's identity."

As far as Val knew, that was a new twist. "What lengths?"

"Cut off her fingertips."

Val's fingers ached in response.

"Took a baseball bat to her face."

Her cheekbones could almost feel the blows.

"And he… uh, he removed her teeth. The uppers with the bat, the lowers by taking off her jaw."

Val clamped her teeth together hard.

"I didn't see anything like that in the reports about your murder."

Val shook her head. "No, nothing like that. That makes me wonder if the killer knew her."

"I feel I need to warn you…"

"Warn me? About what?"

"We have a possible victim."

"How does that require a warning?"

"You might know her."

A tightness gripped Val's chest. She'd lost too many people she knew already. If she hadn't talked to her niece Grace this morning, she'd probably be suffering a full-on panic attack right now. "You have an I.D.?"

"Nothing official. Not yet. But a woman went missing yesterday, and…"

"A woman I know?" Val thought for a moment. She hadn't been invited to the wedding, but a congratulatory card had been circling through the county sheriff's department. "Bobby Vaughan's fiancée?"

The pained look on Stan's face confirmed her guess. "So you do know her. Sorry."

"I've met her, but no, not really. Bobby Vaughan was the lead on our Jane Doe case, though. Until yesterday. Small world."

"You don't know how small. Vaughan's assault and his wife-to-be's abduction? I'm running point on that investigation."

"Busy man."

"Tell me about it. I first pegged Diana Gale as a suspect, the way she disappeared and all. But now…"

"Now you think this might be her."

"She has the same hair color and same build as the body you're about to see. And that's not all."

They followed a bend in the trail. A clearing opened before them. Floodlights highlighted twisted branches of oak. And hanging from one of the thick branches of the largest tree was a woman's bloody body, head down, tied by the ankles.

Like a crime scene photo straight out of the past.

Val approached the body, noting each of the cuts Harlan had demonstrated on her dinner.

"Thoughts?" Stan Perreth finally said, breaking the silence.

"I'm glad you called," Val managed to push from dry lips. The probability that their copycat killer had now taken at least two victims they knew of was disturbing enough. The thought that this woman might be Bobby Vaughan's fiancée was too personally tragic to contemplate. "What else makes you think this might be Diana Gale?"

"Diana was part of a long-term research project at the university. And at various times, that project included interviews with Ed Dryden. Interviews she conducted."

"You think he might have directed this from prison?"

"A woman visits him and then ends up dead? In just the way he liked to kill his earlier victims? Seems possible, doesn't it?"

Val felt sick to her stomach. "Has Bobby Vaughan regained consciousness?"

"Last I checked, they were keeping him under."

"Does Diana Gale have family? Someone who can help with DNA?"

"As a matter of fact, she does. A twin. She came to Madison for the wedding and she's still here."

"Good. How about the university study?"

"I'm in touch with the professor running it."

"And the FBI?"

"I have a call in."

Val pulled out her phone, took several shots of the body and the surrounding area, and traded phone numbers with Stan Perreth.

"Want to go with me to talk to the twin? I could use a woman's touch."

Death notifications, whether Diana was actually dead or

not, were one of the worst parts of a law enforcement officer's job. And if Val could no longer have the best parts, she was sure not volunteering for the worst. "I'm afraid you're on your own for this one."

"Coward."

Val gave him an apologetic shrug.

Besides, she had a stop to make. And broaching the subject of Ed Dryden with the person she was about to visit was going to be tough enough for one night.

Bryce

Bryce held the door and ushered Sylvie out of the building. The cool slap of autumn felt refreshing after the stifling heat inside. He peered down the vacant slope of Bascom Hill stretching down to Library Mall and onward to State Street, and eventually the glowing white dome of the state capitol.

It was a beautiful night. Too bad they couldn't enjoy it.

"Do you think it's possible?"

For a moment, Bryce thought Sylvie had been reading his thoughts. Then reality came crashing back. "That Ed Dryden is behind Diana's disappearance?"

"There's no way he could have that kind of reach in the outside world, is there? I mean, if he was involved in organized crime, that would be another thing. But he's just one man."

Bryce had thought the same thing, before Tanner's death.

"I mean, Sami Yamal seemed pretty bitter," Sylvie went on. "Maybe he kidnapped Diana to discredit Bertram."

"Seems like there are easier ways for him to do that."

"Or maybe Bertram did it."

"She was helping him with his research. He has no reason to want her to disappear."

She blew out a stream of air in frustration. "Well, he seems like a more likely candidate than a serial killer who is behind bars."

"You're scared."

She didn't say a word, just started walking faster.

"It's okay to be scared, Sylvie. I'd be worried if you weren't. Dryden is a scary guy."

"Are you scared?"

"Yes."

"Then why go out of your way to help me? Why not walk away?"

"What do you mean?"

"Smuggling that folder out of Diana's. Coming with me to talk to Bertram. You didn't have to do any of that. Nothing is keeping you here. If you're scared, why not walk away?"

He wasn't sure if he was that transparent or if she was trying to convince herself his real motive had nothing to do with *actually* helping her. "I told you, I have to talk to Diana—"

"About your case, yeah, yeah. Must be an important case."

"It is. But that's not all. I also don't want something bad to happen to your sister. No matter what, she doesn't deserve that."

"You think she is one of those women who are attracted to serial killers—a groupie—don't you?"

"I don't know what you want me to say."

"You do."

"Probably."

She dropped her gaze to the leaves scattering under her feet. With her eyes cast down and anxiety digging lines in her smooth complexion, she looked frustrated, hopeless. "It doesn't seem like her at all."

"Your sister was playing a dangerous game when she entered that prison to interview Ed Dryden."

Sylvie shook her head. "He's in prison. Behind bars. How could he hurt her? Psychologically?"

"Definitely. There's also a chance he has help on the outside."

Sylvie wrapped her arms around her middle and shivered.

Even though he knew her chill was more psychological than physical, he shrugged out of his wool overcoat and draped it around her shoulders.

She held up a hand. "Thank you, but I'm fine."

That stubborn streak again. Stubbornness that only made him want to help her more. What did that say about him? "It's cold. Take it. It's the least I can do."

Grudgingly, she grasped the lapels, pulled the coat around her, and continued walking.

"Thank you."

"For what?"

"Accepting my coat. You're saving me from all the guilt I would feel watching you shiver."

"I'm not used to... stuff like this."

"No kidding."

She shot him a frown. The breeze blew a strand of blond against her cheek.

Bryce stared straight down the hill and quickened his pace. He shouldn't even be noticing the way the wind blew her hair. Not if he wanted to keep his focus where it belonged.

"You said you saw the prison's visitor logs. Who else visited Dryden? Besides Diana?"

"In the last six months? Just your sister and Dryden's attorney."

"If someone is relaying messages for him, maybe it's his attorney."

Her suggestion was so ironic, it took a second for Bryce's brain to rattle back into place. "Impossible."

"Why?"

"I know his attorney. Or his *former* attorney now. The guy's an egotistical bastard, but he'd never be Dryden's lackey. Trust me."

"Are you sure there's no one else?"

"Sure, there's someone else. Prison guards. Other inmates. Any of them could have delivered a message for him."

Sylvie checked her watch. "Damn, it's late already."

"You have plans?"

"I want to go to the hospital, check on Bobby."

When they reached the footbridge arching over Park Street, Sylvie stopped and spun to face him. "What if we're looking at this from the wrong angle entirely?"

She'd lost him. He was still recovering from her attorney question. "What do you mean?"

"What if this doesn't have anything to do with Ed Dryden or Diana? What if *Bobby* was the real target in the attack?"

"So why kidnap her?"

"To hurt him? Say there's someone with a grudge against Bobby..."

She was grasping at straws again, and the path of her thoughts became as clear as if she'd drawn them on a map. "You're thinking about Detective Perreth."

"For whatever reason, he seems to hate Bobby. They worked together, I guess. So let's say Perreth wants to get back at him for something. What better way than to attack him and kidnap Diana? God, he's even trying to blame the whole thing on her. That would really tear Bobby apart."

Bryce figured Sylvie wouldn't want to hear it, but he had to speak up anyway. "Seems a little extreme."

"Why? Because he's a cop?"

"For starters."

"Some cops think the law doesn't apply to them."

"Maybe some do. But I haven't met them. And I've dealt with a lot of cops."

"Maybe you've only dealt with good ones. There are bad people out there too. And some of them are cops."

"Listen, I agree that Perreth is no gem. But I still think Diana's connection to Ed Dryden is too strong to ignore."

"You're probably right. But I'm not discounting any possibilities." She raised her chin. Her lower lip appeared to quiver slightly, but she caught it between her teeth before he could tell for sure.

The gesture dug into Bryce's chest like a dull and rusty blade. What was he thinking? Ed Dryden wasn't the only possibility. There were others. One came to mind immediately. "You know, of the people we talked to today, I'd be inclined to believe Red is our best bet."

"Louis Ingersoll?" Sylvie's brows pulled together. "He *likes* Diana."

"A little too much, don't you think?"

"You think he was stalking her?"

Bryce shrugged. "When she disappeared, she was about to marry another man—a man Ingersoll didn't think was worthy of her."

Sylvie looked up at him with wide eyes. "*If* Perreth is as innocent as you say—and that's still an if in my mind—do you think he knows about Louis?"

"I'll give him a call."

"Thank you."

"Not a problem."

"I mean really. Thank you. I know you don't have to help me with any of this. And I know I don't say it much. But I've really appreciated it."

"So is that thanks a way of telling me goodbye or will you let me drive you to the hospital?"

Sylvie paused for a moment, then broke into a wisp of a smile that made the night even more beautiful. "Why not? You're cheaper than Uber."

SYLVIE

Sylvie convinced Bryce to drop her off, park the car, and try to call Perreth at least once more before risking probable cell phone interference within the hospital.

Really, she just wanted a few moments alone.

As it worked out, she had more than a few. Two of the three elevators were closed for repairs during the late hours, so instead of waiting for the remaining one, she'd climbed five flights of stairs to the ICU. Once there, she was stopped at the nurse's station by a uniformed police officer.

"And you are…" he said.

"Bobby's sister-in-law. Or at least, I was supposed to be. He and my sister…"

The officer gave her a kind smile. "Do you have identification with you?"

"Yes." She dug in her purse, finally locating her Illinois driver's license. Wincing at the awful picture, she handed it to the officer.

After examining it, the officer turned her over to a nurse

who warned her that Bobby had been put into a medically induced coma, led her into a cubicle separated from the rest of the ICU, and pulled a curtain across the open door.

Sylvie had thought she was prepared.

She was wrong.

Swathed in white, with tubes snaking everywhere, black hair shaved clean, and face pale and lifeless as wax, Bobby barely looked human. It was as if the Bobby she knew had disappeared right along with Diana.

Sylvie touched a spot of skin on his hand that was IV-needle free. She'd heard stories about how people in comas could hear, just not respond. She knew she should talk to him. Say something. But she had no idea what. She had no good news to tell him. And if he really *could* hear her, he didn't need to know the bad.

"Ms. Hayes?" A woman in a white coat pulled the curtain aside and stepped into the cubicle. "I'm Dr. Afton."

After some hand shaking and a few pleasantries Sylvie didn't have the patience for, the doctor got down to business.

"Tests indicate we were able to stop the bleeding in his brain," the doctor explained. "I don't expect long-term problems, but we're still watching him carefully at this point."

"When will he regain consciousness?"

"The best thing for him to do is to sleep and heal. If everything continues to go well, it shouldn't be too much longer."

Tears stung Sylvie's eyes. She'd never really thought of Bobby as family, but that's what he would be right now if the wedding had gone as planned.

God knew he'd gone out of his way to include her and to encourage her and make her feel she belonged, as much as possible anyway. When Diana had walked into her life, Sylvie had gained not only a sister, but a brother. An actual blood-related family.

And now she might lose it all.

"Will you have someone call me when he wakes up? I left my number at the nurses' station."

"Of course." The doctor glanced at her watch and stepped toward the curtain.

"Thank you."

A nurse padded in on rubber soles as the doctor slipped out. "Ms. Hayes, we received a call at the nurses' station that you're to meet someone in the lobby. A Bryce Walker?"

"Thanks." Why hadn't Bryce come up? Had he found out Perreth had arranged for Bobby to have police protection and just wanted to give her time alone? Or was it something else?

Sylvie turned back to the bed, embarrassed by how relieved she felt to have a reason to leave. "I'm sorry, Bobby. I'm not very good at this kind of thing. But everything's going to work out. I'll make sure of it."

She walked out of the ICU and down the long hall. Barely glancing at the disabled elevators, she headed directly for the stairs. She pulled the steel stairwell door open. The odor of new paint hit her again, just as strong as it had on her trip up.

Seemed as though the whole city was undergoing some kind of construction, a frantic last push before winter set in.

Sylvie started down the stairs. As she reached the bottom of the first flight, a thunk from above echoed off cement walls. Apparently, someone else was as impatient as she was, paint smell or no.

She continued down the next flight. Above, the sound of footsteps echoed her own. Perfectly matched. As if whoever had entered the stairwell was doing it on purpose.

No, that was ridiculous.

Wasn't it?

Of course, it was. Paranoia was setting in big time. Not surprising after all she'd been through in the last few hours, but ridiculous nonetheless. Still…

Sylvie slowed her pace.

The footsteps slowed, still matching hers.

She speeded up, circling the landing.

The footsteps accelerated, too.

Was someone playing games with her?

No. Couldn't be. She was in a public building, not some haunted house from a horror flick. Even though it was late, she could open the door on any floor and rejoin civilization. She stopped in her tracks.

Above her, the footfalls stopped.

Her breathing rasped in her ears. "Who's there?"

Her question echoed against concrete walls.

No answer.

"Is anyone there?"

Again, nothing.

Sylvie looked back at the door, several steps above. What kind of a person would try to attack someone in a public building? Just a few steps away from help?

Whoever had taken Diana from her own wedding, that's who.

Sylvie looked down the stairwell. Reaching the next floor was her best bet. Once there, she could find help. Whoever was following wouldn't dare attack her in a hallway bustling with people.

Taking a deep breath, she launched into a run. Her shoes clattered on concrete. She reached the mid-floor landing. Gripping the handrail, she whipped around the turn and headed down the next staircase.

Footsteps drummed above her. Faster. Keeping time.

Ohmygod, ohmygod, ohmygod.

Sylvie hit the landing and grabbed for the doorknob. She yanked the door open and lunged out of the stairwell.

And into silent dusty darkness.

Sylvie willed her eyes to adjust to the lack of light. In the red glow of the exit sign above the stairwell door, she could see a hallway set up identically to the ICU floor, a short hallway splitting off the main one, the bank of elevators. But that's where the similarities ended. The level she was on was a mess. Giant power tools cluttered the space, each a hulking shape in the darkness. Dust shrouded the tile floor, slick under her shoes.

The floor was closed for remodeling. And being a weekend night, there wasn't a soul around.

Her throat constricted, making it hard to catch her breath. She had to get off this floor. She had to find people, to find Bryce.

But the *first* thing she had to do was to hide.

She dashed to one side of the hall, ducking behind one hulking obstacle, then another. A pallet of tile. An oversize trash bin. When she reached what appeared to be some kind of table saw, she heard the door of the stairwell open.

Sylvie crouched behind the saw. She didn't dare move. Didn't dare breathe. She thought she was going to be sick.

The door closed with a thud. Soft footsteps scraped across the floor.

She peeked around the table saw, trying to get a look at who was walking toward her. But she could see nothing but more hulking shapes, more red-tinged darkness.

One more step.

Another.

A construction area had to have tools lying about. Didn't

it? If she could find something, anything, she could use as a weapon...

Sylvie groped along the dusty floor with one hand. Her fingers hit slick plastic. A section of PVC pipe. Not anywhere near heavy enough to cause damage, but at least it was something. She wrapped clammy fingers around the pipe.

And waited.

Footsteps scraped closer.

A drop of sweat trickled over her temple. Dust tickled her nose and clogged her throat. She held her breath.

The footsteps halted on the other side of the saw. A hulking figure silhouetted against the red glow. The outline of a man. He was not too tall, but his broad shoulders suggested strength.

Much more strength than she could overpower with a piece of plastic pipe.

Sylvie listened to his breathing, trying to sense the direction of his gaze. An eternity ticked by. Her lungs screamed for air. Her sinuses burned with the need to sneeze.

Finally, he pivoted and walked back the way he'd come. The door to the stairwell squeaked open and then slammed with a bang.

A tremble seized Sylvie's chest. She sagged forward, bracing herself on the saw. Slowly she convinced her fingers to release the pipe, setting it quietly on the floor. But other than that, she didn't dare move.

After a few more minutes she peered around the equipment she was hiding behind. She still could see nothing in the exit sign's light but the tile palettes and various tools, but she was pretty sure she was alone. She waited a minute longer, maybe two, just to be sure.

When she finally stood, her legs tingled and stung as

blood rushed back into them. Stifling a sneeze, she looked down the dusty hall. There had to be another exit, didn't there? Another stairwell? She didn't dare try the one he'd left through.

She stumbled down the dark hallway, rounded the corner, and spotted another red exit sign, glowing like a beacon. Slipping into the stairwell, she raced down the steps to the lobby level.

The light music of human voices greeted her. She pushed through the door, sprinted to the lobby, and spotted Bryce.

"Where have you been?"

"I'm fine. I'm fine." Her knees wobbled.

"What happened?"

She told him.

"Are you hurt?" Bryce looked down at her hands.

Sylvie followed his gaze. Her palms and the knees of her jeans were covered in dust and grit. "No, no, just dirt. I'm okay."

"Did you get a look at him?"

"Not really. It was dark, but..."

"But what?"

"It wasn't Louis Ingersoll. The man I saw was bigger. Not as tall as you, but broad. Strong."

"Why didn't you stay in the ICU?"

"What do you mean?"

"I went up there. You'd left."

"You called the nurses' station. You told me to meet you down here."

He opened his mouth, a stricken look on his face. "I didn't."

"Then who did?"

"Walker?" a gruff voice said from behind them.

Sylvie and Bryce both jumped. Stepping out of Bryce's grip, Sylvie turned and looked into Detective Perreth's bulldog face.

Bryce stepped toward him. "About time you checked your voicemail."

"Voicemail?"

"I left you half a dozen messages. You didn't get the calls?"

"I haven't had time to check my phone."

"Then why are you here?"

Perreth's eyes shifted to Sylvie. "I need you to come with me."

Bryce stepped between her and Perreth. "As her attorney..."

"You can come along. Fine. Whatever you want." The detective swung his focus to Sylvie. His gaze looked so flat, so dispassionate, it made her shiver. "We need your help to identify a body."

Sylvie stared at him. He couldn't be saying what she thought he was. He couldn't. "Diana?"

"That's what we need to find out. Come with me." Perreth led them into a small family waiting room and gestured to a group of chairs. "Have a seat."

Sylvie remained on her feet. Even the thought of sitting, of allowing her body to be so passive, smacked of giving up. She couldn't believe Diana was dead. The buzz in her ears that had become her constant companion the past few hours was still going strong. Wouldn't that have changed if her sister was dead? Wouldn't she feel nothing?

Bryce stood next to her. She could feel him watching her, but he didn't speak. It was as if he sensed she couldn't handle kind words right now. As if he understood nothing could possibly soothe her.

"When can I see her?" she asked Perreth.

"First things first, Ms. Hayes. Really, why don't you take a seat?"

"I don't want to take a seat. I want to see her."

"Seeing her won't do any good."

"I thought you said you needed me to make an identification."

"DNA?" Bryce asked.

Perreth nodded. "Just a swab of your cheek."

Sylvie looked from one man to the other. She didn't just want to give a DNA sample. She needed to see the body. If her senses were wrong—the buzz in her ears, the pinch at the back of her neck, the feeling that Diana was still alive—she needed to know. "I have to see her for myself."

"I'm sorry. That's not possible."

"Why?"

Perreth grunted. "You wouldn't recognize her."

Sylvie shook her head, not wanting to let the implications of his words sink in.

"Dental records?" Bryce prompted.

"I'm afraid that won't help, either."

She couldn't let herself imagine the horror. "What makes you think it's my sister?"

"Height, build, what's left of the hair—all match. And she's the only missing person we have fitting that description. We need your DNA to be certain."

"But you don't know it's her."

"No."

Diana was still alive. She had to be. "How long will the DNA match take?"

"Our lab will expedite. But the time depends on a number of factors. I can't be any more specific than that."

Specific? He hadn't been specific about anything since she met him. "You'll still look for Diana while you're waiting for the results?"

That bored look again. And no answer.

What little oxygen was in the room seemed to leech away. "You can't stop looking for her. Please."

"If she's still out there, we'll find her."

"She isn't dead. She's my twin. I'd know. I'd feel it."

Perreth glanced at her sideways.

She turned to Bryce. "She's not dead."

He reached out and took her hand in his, giving her something to hold on to. "Okay. Then no matter what the police do, we keep looking."

Tears pressed hot against the backs of her eyes and burned through her sinuses. She was so afraid, so very afraid she would never see her sister again. But Bryce was here with her. And though she could tell he feared she was wrong, that deep down he probably believed Perreth, he was willing to listen, willing to help.

And more solid than anything she'd ever known.

Bryce

After Detective Perreth swabbed Sylvie's cheek to get a DNA sample, they told him about Louis Ingersoll's strange behavior, Diana's visits to the prison, and Sylvie's frightening experience in the hospital. The detective seemed to listen, took a few notes, and said he'd ask patrol officers to drive by Sylvie's hotel every couple of hours.

At least it was something.

By the time Bryce walked Sylvie back to her hotel room, it

was well past midnight, and he felt wearier than sleep could ever cure.

He could never make up for his decision to represent Dryden. He could never wash Tanner's blood from his hands. And now, if Diana Gale was indeed lying in the morgue, he would have her blood to contend with too.

He eyed Sylvie as she walked beside him. He couldn't change the past. Couldn't erase what he'd done. All he could do now was to help her either find her sister or face her grief.

"Do you have someone I could call? Someone to stay with you?"

"No."

"No one?"

Reaching the door, she fumbled in her pocket for the keycard. "I'll be fine. Really."

Like hell she would. She might have insisted her sister wasn't dead, but that didn't mean she wasn't scared out of her mind that it was true. She hadn't yet shed a tear, but the dam holding her emotions would crack eventually. When it did, she was going to need someone to turn to, someone to help her through it.

Bryce had no business being that person. Hell, he'd more than proved he wasn't good at thinking of others. His single-mindedness had been a plus in the world of law, not so in the area of personal relationships. He couldn't count the times he'd let his mother down. And Tanner...

But he couldn't just walk away.

"Would you like me to stay? For a little while at least?" The words were out of his mouth before he could bite them back.

"I can't ask that."

"You didn't ask. I offered." He waited for her to push him away, as she'd done since they met.

Instead, she dipped her chin. "Thanks."

He followed her into the room. It looked the same as it had hours before, but it seemed everything had changed since then. The mood. The heaviness of the air. Him. The last time he'd entered this room, he'd been looking for a way to prove Diana was a murderess. Now he clung to the hope that she wasn't a victim.

He turned to bolt the door. When he turned back, Sylvie was still standing in the center of the room, arms hanging limp by her sides. She glanced around as if unsure where to go, what to do next.

"Sit. I'll get you something to drink."

She sank onto the loveseat.

Booze would be good. Just a little to take the edge off. Unfortunately there was no minibar in the room, so he settled for tap water in a plastic cup.

She gripped it with both hands and brought it to her lips. After two swallows, she lowered it. "Thank you."

"Maybe I should run down to the hotel bar for some whiskey."

She shook her head absently, as if his words didn't register. "I do have friends you know. The people I work with at the restaurant, my neighbors, stuff like that. But they're the kind of friends you chat with, maybe drink with after work. That's the kind of friends I have. That's the only kind of friends I really wanted."

"Why?"

She shrugged a shoulder, as if to show it really didn't matter.

But it didn't take a psychiatrist to see how much it did.

"Because that kind of friend will never—how did you put it?—leave you in the lurch?"

"Everyone will leave you in the lurch sooner or later. With that kind of friend, it just doesn't hurt as much."

"You're kind of young to be that cynical."

"I was a foster child, remember?"

He took a seat beside her. "Why was your sister adopted and you weren't?"

"There aren't a lot of families who want to take on a sick toddler."

"You were sick?"

"My heart wasn't fully developed when I was born. At least, that's what I was told."

"Did you live in a lot of different foster homes?"

"Not as many as some kids do."

"But?"

"I guess I just always had the sense that I didn't belong. That they were taking care of me, but they weren't my real family, you know?"

He didn't know. But then, how could he? He'd grown up with his parents hovering over him, and his little brother teasing him and breaking his toys. He'd always known he belonged. "It must have been hard."

"Only the first time."

"What happened the first time?"

"It's not important."

"They left you..."—he paused for a moment, trying to remember exactly how she'd put it— "...in the lurch?"

"You could say that, I guess. She got pregnant."

"So what happened to you?"

"At first, they included me in everything." Sylvie smiled a little. "Watching her belly grow. Shopping for the crib and baby clothes. I even got to pick out these little washcloths shaped like a duckling and an elephant. They fit over your hand like a puppet. I was so excited about giving the baby a bath with those."

Her smile faded.

"What happened?"

"The child services people came to get me a couple weeks before the due date. I never got to see the baby." She shook her head, as if she still couldn't understand it, as if she still felt the sting. "They let me get all excited picking out washcloths knowing I'd never get to use them."

"How could someone do that to a kid?"

"Other kids went through worse. I was actually very lucky."

Lucky. Right. If having your heart broken as a child was lucky. "Did you find another family?"

"I was bounced around. But it didn't hurt. Not like that first time. You learn not to let it."

"How could it not hurt?"

"That's the secret of cynicism. It's strong. Like a suit of armor." Although her eyes were dry, she brushed them with the back of her hand. "They say you should be grateful for the time you have with someone. But I've never been able to do that."

Bryce knew she wasn't just talking about her first foster family. She was talking about her sister. "I'm not known for being grateful, either."

Sylvie searched his eyes.

"I lost my brother recently."

"I'm sorry. I didn't know."

Of course, she didn't. She didn't know anything about him. But for some reason, he wanted her to. At that moment he wanted her to know everything. "I had twenty-nine years with my brother. And all I feel is anger that he's gone."

"How did he die?"

"It was ruled a hunting accident, but…"

"You don't agree?"

"He was murdered. I just can't prove it."

"I'm so sorry, Bryce. Is that the case you're working on? The one you thought Diana could help you with?"

"Yes."

"How could Diana help?"

"I… I think I was wrong about that."

He needed to tell Sylvie the rest. But something stopped him. It seemed cruel to delve into the story of Tanner's death just as she was waiting to hear if her sister had suffered the same fate. Probably at the hands of the same man. And if Bryce was being honest with himself, he'd admit that the part of him that agreed to represent Ed Dryden was a part he never wanted Sylvie to know.

"Are your parents still living?" Sylvie asked.

"My mother is. She lives in a skilled-care facility here in town. But she doesn't really remember Tanner, or me. His death never registered." A fact for which he *was* grateful.

"I'm so sorry." Sylvie slipped a hand over his. Her skin was so warm, so soft.

The ache in his gut spread into his chest. He hadn't talked to anyone but Tanner about their mother's illness. How her memories had slipped away, bit by bit, until she hadn't even recognized her sons anymore. "I visit her, even though she doesn't know who I am. I take her for walks, pretend she's still there. She loves looking at the gardens. She's never forgotten her love of flowers."

Sylvie watched him, her expression soft and sad. As if she was absorbing his heartache and making it her own.

As if she needed more.

"I don't want to talk about my mother."

"Why not?"

"I stayed to help you."

"You are helping me. Talking is helping me."

He looked at her dubiously.

"I'm sure your mother remembers you. Somewhere deep, I'm sure she senses you're special. I think it's like that with family."

"You're not so cynical, after all."

She shrugged. "I have my moments."

Bryce smiled. "Maybe she does have some idea, however vague. Some days I like to think so."

"I'm sure of it. Families just get used to taking those feelings for granted. That connection. But that doesn't mean it's not there." Her lips curved in a wistful smile. "Tanner. That's a nice name."

It sounded nice when she said it. "He was a great guy, for a little brother."

"How much younger?"

"Three years. But he might as well have still been a kid collecting strays. I think he lived for pro bono work." The ache inside Bryce grew, filling his body and mind until it hurt to breathe. He'd tried so hard *not* to remember how it used to be with Tanner, with his mom. He'd focused on everything else—investigating Tanner's murder, building a case, plotting revenge—all so he didn't have to feel this kind of pain. To acknowledge his guilt. To recognize he was now alone in the world. As alone as Sylvie.

The only difference was that he deserved it.

He shook his head. "I'm sorry. I didn't stay to relive my own regrets."

"Not all your memories are regrets."

He hadn't realized that, but she was right.

"You helped me, too," she said.

"I don't see how."

"By showing me it's possible to survive, to go on, even if..." She shook her head. "You know, even if I'm alone again."

Bryce knew he shouldn't touch her, but he couldn't help it. Slipping an arm around her shoulders, he gathered her close. Her body felt warm and delicate. Her hair smelled like spiced flowers. He soaked her in, as if absorbing her essence would fill that empty place inside him... and blot out all he knew about himself.

"You're not alone, Sylvie."

Pivoting toward him, she buried her head in the crook of his neck. Her body trembled against his side and the first trickle of tears seeped into his shirt collar.

Sylvie

Sylvie closed her eyes. Bryce's embrace felt so good, so right, she wanted to soak it in. But she also knew it couldn't last.

She stepped back, out of his arms. "I'm sorry. I'm sorry. I didn't mean to get so upset."

"That's not something you have to be sorry about."

"Well I am. And thank you for staying, but I'm okay now."

Bryce crooked an eyebrow. "You're back to getting rid of me again?"

"It's late."

He glanced at his watch. "Oh, I didn't realize... Listen, I'll see you first thing in the morning."

"I've already taken enough of your time."

"You *are* trying to get rid of me." Bryce tilted his head as if to study her from another angle. "We're supposed to be working together. I thought we agreed. What's wrong?"

"Nothing."

"Not buying it."

Sylvie didn't want to dwell on her feelings. Not tonight, at least, when she was teetering so close to tears. But she supposed Bryce deserved an explanation, so she'd do her best to give him something.

"I guess... I just don't believe..." There it was, the burn she felt in her sinuses, a warning that tears were on their way.

"You don't believe... what?"

How could she explain? "There's just something... Something I always come back to."

"What?"

"Why are you really helping me?" she finally blurted. "And don't give me some line about a confidential case. I really need to know."

He paused.

Debating how much to tell her? Or coming up with a story? Sylvie wasn't sure.

"I'm representing the family of one of Ed Dryden's victims."

Sylvie's stomach hollowed out. Tears felt as if they were pressing at the backs of her eyes. She felt Diana was still alive —she really did—but what if she was fooling herself? "And you believe Diana is also a..."

"I believe Diana might be able to give me some insight into Dryden. That's why I want to help you find her."

Sylvie's knees wobbled a little. "So you think she's alive."

"You said you felt she was."

"I do."

"Then why would I doubt that?"

Sylvie's knees wobbled a lot.

"You still don't believe me?" he asked.

"It's not that. I'm just..."

"Relieved?"

She nodded. "I was afraid I was fooling myself."

"Perreth admitted he had no evidence it was Diana."

"I know."

"So we continue looking, right?"

Sylvie nodded.

"But... Hell. I need to be straight with you. Finding your sister isn't the only reason I want to help."

Sylvie knew it. There was more. Bracing herself, she nodded for him to continue.

"I like you."

She looked down, studying the bland hotel carpet.

"I mean it. I can't pretend I'm only here for my case or because you and I made a deal. I like being with you."

He slipped an arm around her.

Sylvie looked up at him, searching his eyes. She'd wanted the truth, but this wasn't what she had in mind.

Was it?

If it wasn't, she should say so. She should explain that she didn't do relationships, that they were too risky, that she wasn't interested. Instead she waited, barely breathing, trying to see herself in his eyes.

Bryce lowered his mouth to hers. He brushed his lips over Sylvie's lightly, with more sweetness than passion, more caring than lust, more searching than claiming. But the fire his kiss ignited burned to her toes.

She couldn't let herself want this. Couldn't let herself take that step to the edge. Placing her hands against his chest, she gently pushed him away. "I... I can't do this."

"I'm sorry. I was out of line." But he didn't look like he thought he was out of line. He looked like he wanted to kiss her again.

And she wanted it too.

Jitters seated themselves low in her belly. "I... I have to go to sleep."

"Of course. First thing in the morning then? I'll bring donuts."

"Boston cream?"

"A woman after my own heart." He walked to her hotel room door.

"Bryce?"

Hand on the knob, he turned back.

"It's... it's just not a good time. Okay?"

He gave her a nod, as if he understood. "I hope there will be a good time. Someday."

"I..." Sylvie's voice trailed off. She felt out of breath. Exhilarated. Scared to death. As if she was at the pinnacle of a mountain.

And was about to jump.

"...I hope so, too."

Val

Val watched the last patron of The Doghouse drive out of the gravel parking lot. She'd been dreading this since she'd left the crime scene in Madison, but now that the tavern was closed, she was out of excuses.

She pushed herself out of the car, forced her legs to carry her to the entrance, and tried the door. It opened easily.

The tavern looked shabby, as always. A scarred pool table in the middle of a worn, hardwood floor. The smell of stale beer in the air. An old Eagles song playing on an even older jukebox.

"We're closed," a female voice shouted from the back room.

"I'm not here for the booze."

"Then tell me you're dying to scrub the toilets, or I'm not interested." Nikki Sinclair bustled into the main room, a cigarette pinched between her lips. Her shoulder-length hair looked different every time Val saw her, tonight's 'do a light shade of pink that resembled both the color and texture of cotton candy.

"I need your help," Val said.

"Need money?"

"No." Val scowled. She'd never gone to Nikki for money.

"Need to get laid?"

"No." That was even more outrageous.

"Sex advice, then? The firefighter not working out for you?"

"I'm serious, Nikki. I need your help."

"Why do I not like the sound of that?"

"There's some stuff going on, and the only one who might have real insight on this is you."

The mischievous grin fell off Nikki's face. "Get out of here."

"Nikki, please."

"Get out of here now. I'm not kidding."

"You don't even know—"

"I saw the news. The body."

"Two."

Nikki took a long drag off her cigarette. "So you think you have a serial killer. I can't help with that."

"But you can help. There are things only you would know about—"

"I don't know shit, Val."

"You know about Ed Dryden."

"This isn't about Eddie."

Val paused. She hadn't talked to either Bobby or Perreth about how much detail they'd be willing to disclose to a civilian like Nikki. Val shouldn't be making this call on her own, but she was pretty sure Nikki would rather die than talk to anyone about this particular subject.

Including Val.

"The murders, they share some similarities with the ones Dryden committed," Val finally said.

Nikki gave her a hard stare. "As far as I'm concerned, Eddie is dead."

"Nikki, come on. We think this is a copycat. One who might even be in contact with Dryden. There are women out there... innocent women, and you might be the only one who—"

"Nikki Dryden is dead, Val. I don't see things like she did, not anymore. I'm something now. I have something. I'm not going back."

"I'm not asking you to go back."

"Yes, you are. I can't just take a scalding shower and wash him off. Eddie... he's an infection. He gets in my blood and makes me sick."

"We're not dealing with him. Not really. We just need to

understand how he might think, if he's manipulating someone."

"Listen to yourself. That's Eddie's poison. How he thinks. How he manipulates."

"I'm not asking—"

"That's exactly what you're asking. And I'm saying no. In fact, I'm saying get the hell out of here or I'll call the cops."

"This doesn't have to be that involved, Nikki. Not if you don't want it to. Anything you can give me would be great. Like when is the last time you—"

"I can just imagine it now. Chief Olson dragging you out in cuffs. What a show."

"Please, Nikki. You're the only one who—"

"I'm not the only one. Call my sister. Call her husband, for Christ's sake. He's still doing his little lectures on the evil of Ed Dryden. I've had it with this shit. You and Eddie's lawyer can go fuck yourselves."

"Eddie's lawyer? What about his lawyer?"

"He came around here. Asking questions. Apparently it's the season for assholes who want to rip open my scars."

"What did he ask?"

"Same shit you're working up to, I imagine. When's the last time I heard from Eddie? Would he get himself a disciple on the outside? Do I know who might fit the bill?"

"And what did you tell him?"

"To go fuck himself. Exactly what I'm telling you. But first..." Nikki held out her hand, palm up. "Give me a twenty."

Val dug in her pocket and pulled out a wadded up ten and a five, four ones, and an assortment of change. She forked them over. "I appreciate this."

Nikki made a show of counting the cash. "What? You think you're paying for my expertise here?"

"I'm not?"

"Hell no. This is for the shots it's going to take to get me to sleep tonight, thanks to you. And if the nightmares come back in the middle of the night, you're going to owe me for a bottle."

SYLVIE

Sylvie's cell phone jangled her from a dead sleep. She bolted upright.

Where was she?

What time was it?

Who could be calling?

The details of the day before hit her along with the second ring. Heart pounding, she grabbed the phone in sweat-slicked hands and held it to her ear. "Hello?"

"Ms. Hayes?" A deep voice, calm. Not Bryce. Not Perreth.

"Who is this?"

"Charles Rowe. I'm a resident at the hospital."

Sylvie's heart tripped into double time. "Bobby? Is he okay?"

"Actually, yes. He's asking for you."

"He's awake?"

"He insisted I call. I'm sorry it's so early, but he said it was urgent."

She glanced at the clock. 4:00 a.m. It wasn't even dawn yet. But that didn't matter. Bobby was awake. He was going to be okay. And she could talk to him. "Tell him I'll be right there."

"He'll be happy to hear it."

Sylvie didn't wait for goodbyes. She ended the call, dropped the phone in her purse, and bounded out of bed. She was dressed and out the door in minutes.

Outside the hotel, the lingering glow of a streetlight filtered through orange leaves clinging to the branches of a sugar maple. Her breath puffed in front of her in frosty clouds. Cold poked through her jacket and between the fibers of her sweater, knifing straight to her skin.

For a second, Sylvie toyed with the idea of calling Bryce. After he'd left, she'd spent more than an hour staring at the ceiling, trying to untangle her feelings. She hadn't succeeded. If anything, she'd felt more tempted to fling herself off the emotional cliff and more afraid he wouldn't be there to catch her if she did.

She pulled out her phone, summoned an Uber, and sent a quick text to Bryce, letting him know what was happening. Somehow the idea of him meeting her at the hospital seemed safer, less needy.

The sound of an approaching car cut through her thoughts. She tapped send and looked up from her phone. A white minivan pulled to the curb in front of her. The driver's door opened.

A van. White.

Wait. Was that right?

Sylvie had been so focused on what to text Bryce, she'd hardly noticed the details of the Uber that had committed to picking her up. She pulled up the app, and—

She sensed movement, the driver getting out of the car. She glanced up. Her hair blew in her eyes, obscuring her vision, but she could still make out the driver barreling toward her, broad shoulders decked out in a puffy university jacket, dark eyes staring from a red ski mask.

Her body froze. Her mind scrambled to make sense.

A ski mask? It wasn't cold enough for a ski mask.

A gloved hand clamped around her bicep.

Sylvie spun to the side and pulled back, trying to rip her arm free. Her feet skidded. She went down, her knee smacking the concrete.

His fingers tightened, bruising strong. He yanked her to her feet. Her back slammed against a solid chest. His other arm circled her throat.

Sylvie scratched at his arm, his hands, her fingernails scraping slick nylon and leather. She kicked backward, connecting with a shin.

A muffled grunt vibrated through his chest.

Then his arm pressed against her throat, cutting off her scream.

Bryce

Bryce jabbed the elevator button for the lobby.

Nothing happened.

He jabbed again.

Last night Sylvie had assumed he was driving home, and he'd let her. If she'd known he'd taken a room just down the hall from hers, she probably would have thought he was overreacting. At the time, he would have considered her at least partially right.

But now?

What in the world was she doing leaving the hotel before sunrise? If she hadn't texted, he wouldn't have even known she was gone.

The elevator doors finally closed. It lurched a little, then started to move.

Slowly.

Far, far too slowly.

He should have taken the stairs. But after an excruciating

wait, the doors opened at the lobby level. Bryce dashed out at a barely civilized fast walk. He'd parked in the ramp across the street, so he headed for the hotel's front door and pushed out into the dark.

Except for a circle of yellow light from the streetlight on the far corner, shadows cloaked the block. But even through the darkness, Bryce could make out a white van to the left of the hotel. And the dark silhouette of a man wrestling something into the back.

Not something. Someone.

Sylvie.

"Hey!" Bryce yelled. He launched into a run.

The man looked in Bryce's direction.

Sylvie yanked herself backward, nearly twisting away. She thrashed the man's face with her free hand.

The man pulled back his arm, hand forming a fist. He plowed it into Sylvie's jaw.

Her head snapped back. Her body sagged.

No, no, no.

Bryce pushed himself to move faster.

The man stuffed Sylvie into the back of the van and climbed in after. The door began to slide shut.

Bryce lunged for it. He gripped the steel edge with his left hand. Fighting to gain leverage, he pulled backward.

The door stopped its slide.

Bryce yanked harder, but the door wouldn't open.

A foot shot from the opening and smashed into Bryce's nose.

For a second, the pain stunned him. Then hot blood gushed down his face and filled his mouth. Dizziness swamped him. Bryce shook his head, trying to clear it.

The space narrowed. Steel sandwiched the fingers of his

left hand. Pinching. Crushing. He couldn't let go. If the door closed, Sylvie was gone.

A thump hit the inside of the door. Then another.

Oh, God...

Bryce threw his weight against the door's motion. It again shuddered to a stop, but he couldn't pry it wider.

Something red slammed against the window. A scream and more thuds came from inside. One more yank from Bryce, and the door slid open like a shot and Sylvie tumbled out, head-first.

Bryce half-caught her. He stumbled backwards before landing on the sidewalk, Sylvie on top of him.

Rubber squealed against pavement and the vehicle roared away down the street.

"Bryce!" Tears streamed down Sylvie's swollen face. "He hurt you. Oh, God, you're all bloody."

He bet he looked like a mess. He sure hurt like hell. But it didn't matter. All that mattered was that Sylvie was safe. "Why did he let you go?"

"He didn't."

"Then how?"

"He got between my feet and the door. I guess he was more worried about you than me."

Bryce would have laughed, if his face didn't hurt so much. He could only hope the bastard had a broken rib or two. Share the wealth. "Why don't you let me give you a ride to the hospital, okay?"

Sylvie clambered to her feet and then offered him a hand... until she saw his fingers. "Our first stop should probably be the ER."

When Perreth reached the hospital, they were still sitting in the ER waiting room. Bryce's whole head throbbed, and the fingers of his left hand were as thick and stiff as bratwurst.

A bruise bloomed in a deep shade of pink along Sylvie's swollen jaw. And her eyes held a glassy look—the result of either a concussion or shock, neither one a nice prospect. But apparently their injuries weren't serious enough to warrant the slightest bit of urgency on the part of the ER staff.

Perreth narrowed his beady eyes on Sylvie and cleared his throat with a wet smoker's cough. "Can you tell me what this guy looked like?"

She went over his description: build, clothing, van.

"You're not giving me much to go on," Perreth said. "Should I go out and arrest everyone who drives a minivan and wears a Badgers jacket? Half the Madison population would be in jail."

He had a point. Their description wouldn't get him very far. But Bryce still didn't appreciate the smart-ass tone. Maybe Sylvie's suspicions were rubbing off on him, but even he was beginning to wonder about Perreth's agenda regarding this case.

But then, maybe the detective was just an ass.

"We told you someone was after Sylvie. How about getting her some real protection this time?"

Sylvie turned to look at him, but she didn't protest. Apparently she was a realist when she had to be.

The detective looked at him as if he'd just been jolted from a faraway dream. "Police protection?"

"What other kind?"

"Maybe a little common sense? Starting with not wandering around in the dark. Alone. I had officers driving by the hotel. If she'd just stayed inside…"

"Sylvie wouldn't have gone out alone without good reason." Bryce turned to her. Waiting to hear it himself.

"I got a call from a doctor. He said Bobby was awake and wanted to see me. Have you talked to him yet, Detective?"

Perreth narrowed his eyes on her. "When did you get this call?"

"Right before I left the hotel. Around four this morning."

"And it was a doctor, you say?"

"A resident."

Perreth pulled out a pad and pen. "And this resident, did he give a name?"

"Charles Rowe."

He made another note. A nurse emerged from the swinging door and looked down at her clipboard. "Sylvie Hayes?"

Sylvie reluctantly lifted herself out of the chair. With one last pointed glance in Bryce's direction, she hobbled to the nurse's side and disappeared through the swinging doors.

"So how did you stumble upon this scene?"

"I was there. At the hotel. Sylvie texted me."

Perreth frowned. "If you were there, why did you let her go off alone?"

Bryce knew what the detective was thinking, that he'd stayed with Sylvie last night. Of course, Bryce could only wish that had been true.

He rubbed his forehead, trying to forget the torn look in Sylvie's eyes when he'd kissed her. He shouldn't have done it. Not when there was so much he still hadn't told her. The problem was, even knowing the kiss was a mistake, Bryce still wanted to do it again. "I wasn't staying with her."

"You were just wandering the hotel?"

Did the detective want him to paint a picture?

Bryce blew a frustrated breath through tight lips. He'd had enough of answering Perreth's questions. He needed to ask a few of his own. "Why were you so interested in the call Sylvie got from the resident?"

"Just covering all the bases."

"Right. And that's why you wrote down his name?"

Perreth gave him his trademark bored look and didn't answer.

"I suppose I could ask about the guy around the ICU," Bryce finally said.

"Fine. There is no resident named Rowe caring for Bobby Vaughan."

"What do you mean?"

Perreth looked at him as if he were a bit slow on the uptake. "Exactly what I said. There is no Charles Rowe. Vaughan is under protection. Not everyone in a white coat can just waltz in to examine him."

"So you *are* going to give Sylvie full time police protection, right? Now that you know this guy lured her out of the hotel to kidnap her?"

"I can't give guarantees."

Bryce slapped his hands on his thighs in frustration. The pain made him regret it immediately. "You can't be serious."

"The city budget is serious."

"What more reason do you need? Her dead body?"

"Like I said last night, if she agrees to stay in her hotel, I can send a uniform over to check on her every couple of hours. But that's as much as I can promise."

"What's to keep this guy from attacking her between visits?"

Perreth shrugged. "You seem to be around her a lot."

True. But after last night, that had become a problem.

"In fact, I have to wonder why you're suddenly around her so much."

"That's none of your business."

"None of my business? I thought you were her lawyer. That seems to be connected to my business."

Damn. Bryce had forgotten that he was supposed to be acting as Sylvie's lawyer. The kiss last night, the attack this morning, all of it had thrown him so far off his game, he could no longer keep track of his own rules. "And I have to insist you give my client police protection."

Perreth gave him a knowing smile. "You have some other interesting clients too."

"You've been wasting your time investigating me?"

"Just checking your credentials. I'll bet it was interesting, representing a serial killer."

Bryce felt cold. He'd known it was only a matter of time before someone would look up his history, but still, he wasn't ready. Not for Perreth to throw it in his face, and especially not to have Sylvie find out.

"Lot of publicity in that prison lawsuit. Sylvie see your name on the news? Is that how she decided to hire you?"

"Something like that. None of this is relevant."

"Maybe not. But there are a lot of strange things going on around here. Thought you might like to straighten things out."

"There's nothing to straighten."

"If you say so. Far be it from me to tell a lady how she should pay her legal bills."

"It's not like that."

"Whatever you say. Drive-by checks are all I can offer. Just keep her from sneaking out of bed on ya next time, and she'll be plenty safe. If you can't handle it, let me know."

Bryce caught himself before he let out a big sigh of relief. As long as Perreth was focused on who Sylvie was sleeping with, he wasn't telling her about Bryce's tie to Dryden. And that would give Bryce a little more time to figure out how to tell her himself.

Sylvie

Sylvie looked at Bryce's left hand and winced. Bruises mottled the swollen skin. "Are you sure they're not broken?"

Bryce wiggled his fingers. "See? Not broken."

"How about your nose? That's got to be painful."

Coordinating colors stretched over his puffy nose and darkened the skin under his eyes. "Nothing a few ibuprofen won't fix."

"Didn't they give you anything stronger than that?"

"Didn't need anything stronger." He gave her a reassuring smile. "How about you? Shouldn't they be keeping you here for observation or something?"

She might have a headache sharp enough to split wood, but she wasn't about to fall for his attempt at distraction. She had the feeling his refusal of medication had more to do with the need for a clear head than lack of pain. "I'm fine. That is, I will be when you tell me what happened with Perreth."

"Or maybe you won't be." Bryce glanced toward the door. "Let's get out of here, go back to the hotel. Perreth agreed to send an officer by to check on you every few hours. I'll tell you what else we talked about when we get there."

"Not until I see Bobby."

His lips pinched together in a pale line. "He's still unconscious, Sylvie."

"The doctor called me. He told me..." The tremor inside

turned cold. She pulled her jacket tighter around her shoulders and clutched the fabric together at her neck. "The call was a fake."

Bryce nodded.

Of course, it was. Hadn't she thought the call was strange? Why hadn't she put the pieces together? Was she so eager to talk to Bobby that she would believe anything without question?

"So the man who kidnapped Diana is after me."

"It appears so."

"And he's likely the same man who followed me in the stairwell last night."

"Yes."

"But I've never met Ed Dryden. If he's behind this, why would he be after me?"

"Diana isn't the only one who fits the description of his first victims." Bryce's tone was quiet and matter of fact, but the fear running under it was unmistakable.

The same fear that hummed in her ears. She didn't have to try too hard to conjure up the photos Sami Yamal had shown them. The young blond coeds. Dryden's blond wife—a woman who looked just like Diana, just like Sylvie. "I'm going to go back to Diana's apartment."

"I thought we agreed to stay at the hotel."

"You and Perreth must have agreed. I didn't." She started toward the ER exit. "I'm not going to hole up in my hotel room and wait. I need to find Diana, and the only way I can do that is to look."

"I think Perreth has a point. The hotel is the safest place."

"When did you start listening to Perreth?"

"When he said something that made sense."

"It doesn't make sense to me. We only scratched the

surface of what we might find in Diana's apartment. What if there's more?"

"Don't you think the police would have found it last night?"

"Perreth was looking for something to prove she and Bobby were having problems. I'm betting there is a lot he didn't think was important."

He frowned, as if he wasn't buying the argument.

"I'm not just going to sit around while Diana is still out there somewhere." She started for the exit. "You don't have to go with me, if you don't want."

"Of course, I'm going with you."

It didn't take long to make the drive to Diana's apartment. Sylvie pulled Diana's key from her pocket and fitted it into the lock. Tumblers aligning, she turned the knob and pushed. The door swung open.

A yelp rang from the kitchen. Louis Ingersoll stared at them, eyes wide.

"What are you doing?" Bryce demanded.

"Nothing. I mean, I'm watering the plants." He held up a small pink watering can for proof.

"How did you get in here?" Sylvie asked.

"Diana gave me a key. I take care of the place for her when she goes away."

Bryce stepped toward Louis. "She didn't go away, Ingersoll. She was kidnapped. Only yesterday. I'm sure the plants aren't dry already."

"I just wanted to do something for her."

Sylvie had to admit Louis was a little pitiful in his crush on Diana, but this seemed way over the top. "Are you sure you aren't just snooping around?"

Once again, Louis held up the watering can.

She shook her head. "Why are you really here, Louis? Or would you rather we called the police and you can explain it to them?"

"I swear, I'm not here for any reason. I'm just trying to help. I'm just trying to find her."

"You're trying to help by looking through her things?" Sylvie said.

Louis glanced from her to Bryce and back again. "Well, isn't that why you're here?"

He had them there.

"There's a big difference," Bryce said. "Sylvie is Diana's sister. What are you, Ingersoll? Her stalker?"

"You can't think that I did anything to Diana. I would never hurt her."

Bryce let out a sigh. "That's what all stalkers say."

"I'm not a stalker. I watch out for her. That's all." He looked to Sylvie. "You've got to believe me."

Somehow, she *did* believe him. Louis no longer seemed as sweet to her as he had at first, but she couldn't help but feel he was telling the truth. And besides, if the same man that kidnapped Diana was after her, she'd seen him. Not his face, but his body. And he was a little too tall and much too broad-shouldered to be Louis. "If not you, who?"

"Who is stalking her?"

She nodded. "Who kidnapped her?"

"I don't know."

Bryce took another step forward. He pulled his cell phone from his belt. "You'd better start thinking before I punch in 911."

"There was this guy..."

"Are you making this up just to keep me from calling the police, Louis?"

"No. I swear. There was this guy who kept asking her out. He wouldn't leave her alone. She mentioned him once. I think it was someone she worked with at the university."

Sylvie glanced at Bryce. "Professor Bertram?"

"I don't know his name," Louis said. "But they were working together on the Ed Dryden stuff. The stuff I was helping her with. But I thought he'd finally left her alone when she got engaged to the cop. That's what she told me when I asked her about him. But then about a week ago…"

Bryce leaned forward. "A week ago? What happened?"

"It was weird. I didn't know Diana was busy. I went to the door to knock, and I accidently heard him."

"What did you hear?" Sylvie asked.

"He was upset. Crying."

Bryce scoffed. "You must have accidently had your ear pressed against the door."

Louis threw up his hands. "He was really loud, like sobbing. I didn't have to try very hard to hear him."

Sylvie and Bryce exchanged looks. She nodded for him to continue with his questions while she focused on Louis Ingersoll's eyes, trying to figure out if he was telling the truth.

"Are you sure it was the same guy who was asking her out?" Bryce asked.

"No." Louis returned Bryce's gaze, his voice steady. "But I know the guy who was crying was from the university. I asked her after he left. She said it was someone she was working with on the Ed Dryden research project."

"And that's all she said?"

"Yeah. She didn't want to talk about it more than that. Said it was private."

"Why didn't you tell us this before?"

He shrugged, seeming self-assured, even smug. "Didn't think of it until now."

"Did you tell this to the police?"

"Like I said, didn't think of it. You're the one who brought up stalking," He said to Bryce. "So I got to thinking, maybe that guy was stalking her. Maybe he was sobbing because of her upcoming wedding."

Sylvie brushed the hair back from her face. Was that possible? Could Professor Bertram have been stalking Diana?

Sylvie thought of Mrs. Bertram, her divorce from her husband, the reluctance with which she'd opened the door. Maybe fear wasn't the reason she didn't want to face Sylvie. Maybe the real reason was that Sylvie looked exactly like Diana, the woman her husband was obsessed with.

She glanced at Bryce.

He nodded, as if he'd read her mind. "Let's go see Bertram."

Diana

The shadows in the room grew until there was nothing but darkness. Diana was starving, her throat dry.

He'd left hours ago...

Or had it been minutes?

Diana tried to withdraw into her thoughts, her memories. For comfort. To pass the time. But she couldn't seem to focus on happy times. She'd try to relive road trips with Bobby and wedding planning with Sylvie, even the beautiful but cold house she grew up in, yet her mind would stray to awful images, some she wasn't sure were even real.

Her father reaching under her skirt and pinching her

inner thighs until they were purple with bruises. Then laughing and daring her to tell.

The contempt on Mother's face when Daddy left. Contempt for *her*.

Bobby bleeding.

Bobby dead.

The faces would change in front of her eyes. Interchangeable as Halloween masks. The awfulness playing over and over. Other horrors too. And her not being able to say anything. Not being able to scream. Not being able to help herself at all.

And through all of it, a dark shadow would be standing in the doorway, silently watching. And then gone, gone, gone.

When would he be back?

What would he do then?

And what would become of her if he never came back at all?

Sylvie

After shooing Louis back to his own apartment, Sylvie and Bryce raced the few blocks to the psychology department's temporary digs. Bertram said he worked every day of the week. Sylvie hoped that wasn't an exaggeration.

They reached the top of the stairs and headed down the hall. The air felt different. Colder. They walked past the office where Sami Yamal had shown them the photographs of the women killed by Ed Dryden. Sylvie peered inside. Two people worked at desks in the large room, but Sami wasn't one of them.

Too bad. Sylvie would like to get his take on the professor's relationship with Diana. If there was any impropriety at all where the professor was concerned, she was sure Sami would have noticed. And with no love lost between him and Bertram, he certainly wouldn't worry about keeping the professor's secrets.

The door to the professor's office was closed, just as it had been the first time they'd visited. But unlike the first time, a light glowed from underneath the door.

Bryce knocked. The door swung open under his knuckles.

Professor Bertram stood in the doorway. Dark circles cupped reddened eyes. Razor stubble sparkled silver over his jaw and shadowed the hollows of his cheeks. A spot of coffee about the size of a half-dollar marred his wrinkled blue shirt.

"I thought only students pulled all-nighters, not professors," Bryce said.

"I wish it was as simple as that." Bertram walked back around the desk and collapsed into his desk chair. He ran a hand over his face and looked at Sylvie. "I'm so sorry."

"For what?"

"Your sister."

Her stomach tightened into a knot. "Why?"

"I talked to Detective Perreth. He said he was waiting on an...." He shook his head. "An identification. It never occurred to me she would be in danger. He's in prison. I couldn't have known..."

"Hold on. Hold on," Bryce said. "What exactly did Perreth tell you?"

"He thinks Diana's disappearance might have something to do with Ed Dryden."

Strange. Perreth hadn't even given them a clue that he knew about the link between Diana and Dryden. "Did he say what made him think that?"

"No. But he seemed pretty sure."

Had Perreth found something? Or had he learned that

Dryden was Bertram's weakness and he was using the serial killer to get under the professor's skin?

Sylvie glanced at Bryce.

As if he sensed her unvoiced question, he pulled out his cell phone along with Perreth's card and punched in the number. Stepping into the doorway of the tiny office, he cupped his hand around the phone and started talking in a low voice to whoever had answered the phone. Judging from his polite tone, Sylvie would bet it wasn't Perreth. Maybe the detective's voice mail.

She turned back to Bertram. He really did look stressed. Was guilt over getting Diana involved with Dryden to blame? Or was he stalking her? Or could it be something else? "What was going on between you and Diana?"

Bertram's head snapped up. "What do you mean?"

"Diana's neighbor said you were at her apartment about a week ago." Louis hadn't said it was the professor. Not exactly. But after the scenarios Sylvie's imagination had conjured on the trip over, coming right out and accusing Bertram seemed like the fastest way to get answers.

"We were working together. I stopped by her apartment a couple of times."

"He said he heard you crying. Sobbing, actually."

Elbows on the desktop, he cradled his forehead in his palms.

"What were you upset about?"

He let out a shaky breath. When he looked up, tears sparkled in the corners of his eyes. "It's not what you think."

"You have no earthly way to know what I think." *She* didn't even know what she thought. Not anymore. It seemed everything she thought she knew about her sister had been turned on its head. "What is it?"

"It happened many years ago. Probably not very long after you were born."

Not long after she was born? How could his explanation possibly go back that far? She waited for him to continue.

"I had a daughter. Beautiful girl. Brilliant girl. She was only sixteen when she graduated from high school."

"What does your daughter have to do with Diana?"

He swallowed hard, as if trying to pull himself out of his memories, trying to control his emotions.

"I'm asking you about my sister. I need to know about my sister."

"You asked why I was at her apartment. Why I was upset."

"Yes."

"I'm telling you, if you'd stop and listen." Sad no longer, his dark eyes flashed with temper.

"I'm sorry. Go on."

"My daughter was a student here. I was an assistant professor. I was so proud that she chose to come here. I can't even tell you."

Sylvie forced herself to nod politely even though she felt more like wrapping her hands around his throat and strangling the truth out of him.

"She used to have this book club. Just for fun. She and her friends would get together at a restaurant on State Street and talk about the latest releases. One summer, they drove up north for a weekend, stayed at a girl's parents' cabin. She never made it home. She was found a week later… murdered by Ed Dryden."

Sylvie gasped.

Bryce stepped up close behind her. She hadn't been aware that he'd finished his phone call. But he was there. As soon as she'd gasped, he was there. Before the horror could even take hold.

"That's the real reason I got involved in studying Ed Dryden years later, when Risa Madsen started the program. I had to know why. How he could have done those horrible things to my beautiful little girl. And you know, in all my study, I've never gotten an answer. Not one that made sense. I never found..."

His voice cracked and he buried his head in his hands.

Sylvie let his words sink in. Suddenly his constant work hours made perfect sense. His wife's strange behavior too. Her fear. Her comment about her husband's obsession fit too. He'd been obsessed with Dryden. So obsessed that he'd shut everything else out of his life, including what was left of his family. "I'm sorry, I thought—"

"I know what you thought. That I was a horny old professor hung up on a woman less than half my age."

What could she say? That *was* what she'd thought. That and worse.

"If you're looking for someone who was hung up on your sister, check with my assistant."

"Your assistant?"

"Sami Yamal. I don't think Diana ever actually dated him, but it wasn't for lack of trying on his part. She asked me to have a talk with him a couple of weeks after she started working with us on the project."

"A talk?"

"To suggest that he back off."

Sami? When Louis had told them about the man who'd aggressively pursued dates with Diana and the man who was crying in her apartment, he'd said he couldn't be sure they were the same person. Maybe they weren't.

Heart pumping, Sylvie leaned forward, her palms on the desk. "Is Sami Yamal here today?"

The professor shook his head. "I haven't seen him."

Sylvie's mind raced. Sami was the right size to be her assailant. Had he decided to lay low to hide the bruises she and Bryce must have given him? Or was he with Diana?

"Did he call in sick?" Bryce asked.

"It's Sunday. He often comes in, but he's not required to be here." Bertram raised a shaking hand to his forehead, as if the hassle of answering their questions was too much for him to handle.

Sylvie felt for the man. He seemed so much weaker than the last time they'd seen him, as if the past hours had taken a horrible toll. Losing his daughter to a serial killer had to be the definition of hell. And revisiting that horror would stress the strongest man.

But even if Sami Yamal was the one who had kidnapped Diana and attempted to kidnap Sylvie this morning, even if Diana's disappearance had nothing to do with Dryden, she still couldn't excuse the professor for exposing Diana to that evil in the first place.

No matter how she could sympathize with his need to understand his horrible loss, she couldn't forgive him. "Where does Sami Yamal live?"

Bryce

As soon as they emerged from the building, Sylvie handed Bryce the slip of paper with Yamal's address. Her hand shook. Lines of worry dug into her forehead and flanked her lips.

With the emotional stress she was under, he doubted she needed to be searching down the assistant professor, but he had learned enough about her to realize she had to face him herself. And hell, he could hardly blame her for that.

But he could take precautions. "I'm going to call Perreth, have him meet us at Yamal's apartment."

She shot him an uneasy look, then nodded. "I suppose that's a good idea."

"Perreth is a prick, no doubt about it. But he seems to be doing his job."

"I don't trust him."

"You don't trust anybody."

"You're doing all right. So far, anyway."

Bryce pulled his cell phone from his pocket and squinted down at the slip of paper to hide his smile. He couldn't remember when a heavily qualified half-compliment had meant more.

He punched his phone's redial as they walked down Bascom Hill and left the address on Perreth's voice mail. He sure as hell hoped the detective checked his messages. He didn't want to be stuck facing down Yamal alone.

"How far is Sami's apartment?" Sylvie asked when he finished.

"A fifteen-minute walk up State Street, tops."

Sylvie nodded. "What do you think about Bertram?"

"He seems like a man in pain, like all of Dryden's victims' families." Like him. Maybe like Sylvie, if her sister was dead.

"I don't know how those families coped."

"Who said they coped?" Coping was overrated. Bryce would rather get justice. Or maybe even flat-out revenge.

"Good point." She shook her head and increased her pace. "Somehow, I never really considered Sami might be responsible for Diana's disappearance. I know we talked about it, but he just seemed so helpful that day, so proud of his work."

"When Diana and Professor Bertram arranged to work together, they cut him out of the mix. And if he had unrequited feelings for Diana on top of that..." A clear recipe for disaster. Out-of-control passions always made things more complicated. More volatile.

They crossed the footbridge over Park Street and negotiated their way to Library Mall.

The wind kicked up, blowing blond strands across Sylvie's face. She brushed them out of the way. "I hope Perreth gets there before we do. If Sami hurt Diana, I might just kill him with my bare hands."

Emerging from Library Mall, they crossed Lake Street and started up State in the direction of the capitol dome. Several blocks up, they turned off State Street and located the old Victorian home at the address Bertram had given them. The house had been separated into three flats, each with a separate entrance.

Sylvie poked the buzzer next to Yamal's name.

No answer.

Bryce cupped a sore hand and shielded the window in the door. Through the wavy old glass, he could see a staircase stretching to the second floor. Judging from the stairs, Yamal didn't believe in cleanliness. Tiny muddy cat tracks peppered the old linoleum. And at the base of the stairs, a small orange feline peered at the window and mewed incessantly. "His cat is home."

Sylvie pressed up next to Bryce and peered in. "She seems upset. Do you think something's wrong and she's trying to let us know?"

"Do cats do that?"

"Not a cat person?"

"I don't even have house plants." God, he sounded pitiful. Lonely.

"One of my foster families had a cat. Believe me, when anything was wrong, she'd let you know."

The cat paced back and forth on the stairs without taking its eyes from their faces. Its meow was low, urgent.

Sylvie put a hand on the doorknob and twisted. It turned under her fingers. "My God, it's open."

"Perreth should be here any minute." A trickle of foreboding ran down Bryce's spine. He checked his phone. Nothing. "I hope."

Sylvie pushed the door inward. She stepped inside, stopping at the base of the stairs as the cat wrapped itself around her legs. She bent to stroke the animal's arching back.

The scent hit Bryce through the open door. Sweet. Sort of metallic. Memories of finding Tanner flooded his mind and turned his stomach. "Sylvie. Get out of there."

She turned to him, wide-eyed. "That smell. Is it—"

"Wait for the police."

She turned back to the steps.

He grabbed her arm before she could start up the staircase. Damn, he wished he had a gun, a knife, a baseball bat… anything. "Wait."

"I can't just stand here, Bryce. I have to know." Sylvie tried to pull her arm away.

He held on. "Perreth will be here soon. He has to be."

Where was Perreth?

"Please, Bryce. If that body in the morgue isn't Diana…"

"Don't think that way."

"I can't help it. Imagine how you would feel."

He didn't have to imagine. He'd smelled that odor as soon as he'd opened Tanner's front door. Even though he'd never smelled anything exactly like it before that time, he'd known what the scent was, what it meant. It hadn't stopped him. It hadn't even slowed him down. "Okay, stay behind me."

Bryce slipped his hand down her arm until he gripped her palm in his. Then he started up the stairs, stepping on the edge of the linoleum to avoid walking on the cat tracks—tracks of blood, not mud. "We can't touch anything. This is a crime scene. We can't destroy evidence that might help the police. We shouldn't be going up here at all."

Sylvie's hand trembled in his, but her steps were steady. From the bottom of the stairs, the cat's mewing grew louder, the sound emanating from deep in its throat.

They approached the dark doorway at the top of the stairs. Bryce's eyes drew even with the floor above. More tracks spotted the wood. The smell clogged his throat.

An image crashed through his mind: Tanner's broken body lying in a bed of autumn leaves.

Placing a hand on the door frame, Bryce steadied himself and peered into the apartment. Blood spread over the hardwood floor, not fresh, but brown and sticky. And just inside the archway leading to the kitchen, Sami Yamal stared at them through shattered lenses. A ravaged hole gaped where the top of his skull should be. And in his hand, he still held his gun.

Val

Val had spent half a day in Madison, trying to track down Dryden's former lawyer only to learn he had closed his law firm and put his house on the market, shortly after his brother and partner in the firm had died in a hunting accident. She was already on her way home to her little horse farm outside the town of Lake Loyal when Stan Perreth called.

"You want me to turn around?" she asked, hoping he would say no.

"Yes."

Val let out a heavy sigh. She'd been looking forward to an evening at home with Lund, eating frozen pizza and watching some dumb action movie on Amazon Prime. Probably boring to most, but after this insane weekend, she could use a little downtime and a cuddle on the couch before the official work week started. "Didn't you say it was a suicide?"

"Yes."

"Is there something suspicious about it?"

"Not about the body. At least not that we can tell until the autopsy."

"Then what?"

"I want to run something by you. I'll make it worth your while."

"Fine. I'll be there as soon as I can." Val pulled over to the shoulder, texted Lund, then turned around and headed back in the other direction.

When she finally reached the address Stan had given her, the body had already been taken away. "I thought you wanted to run something by me?"

"Not about the suicide itself. About the guy who committed it." Stan gave her a rundown on Sami Yamal's career and connections.

Val summed it all up. "So, we have a guy who has spent most of his life studying Dryden commit suicide, a woman who has interviewed Dryden disappear, and two recent homicides that mimic Dryden's past murders."

"Exactly."

"And you think they're all connected."

"Don't you?"

"We can't assume anything."

"Oh come on, Val. All of this has gone down at the same time. You think this is a coincidence?"

"No."

Stan gave her a satisfied grunt and then one of his disconcerting smiles.

Val fought the urge to squirm. "We're missing something. The element or elements that tie everything together."

"That's exactly how I see it." Stan reached out and skimmed a finger down her arm. "Why don't we talk about it over dinner?"

"Stan..."

"Come on. We have a lot of work to do, but that's not all there has to be. You have to eat. I have to eat. It could be fun."

Val knew damn well he was no longer talking about dinner. Not really. "My fiancé has dinner waiting for me at home."

"Fiancé?"

Val hated having to trot out Lund as some kind of excuse, but she knew from experience that the mention of another man killed a romantic invitation faster than any woman simply saying she wasn't interested. And she was far too busy to walk the tightrope between firmness in her resolve and bruising Stan's ego.

"I spent the day trying to get in contact with Dryden's lawyer... well, former lawyer."

"Why is that?" Stan said, returning to his usual gruff cop self.

Val was relieved. "He and Diana seem to be the only

names on the prison's visitor record. I thought he might be able to connect some dots."

"I'm sure he can. In fact, he's connected some already."

"You've talked to him?"

"He found Sami Yamal's body."

"What?"

"He was just here. Left less than an hour ago with Diana Gale's sister." Stan gave her a how-do-you-like-me-now grin. "See? We really need to have some dinner."

Val had just opened her mouth to respond when her cell phone rang. Grateful for the moment to collect her thoughts, she fished it out of her pocket and answered. "Ryker."

"Val…" Bobby's voice was weak. "We need to talk."

Sylvie

Sylvie stared at her reflection in the bathroom mirror. Hair tousled and wet and body wrapped in a towel, she looked tired. Shell-shocked. No surprise there. As hard as she tried, she couldn't erase images of Sami Yamal's apparent suicide from her mind. The blood on the floor. The dead stare of his eyes. The smell that had filled her nostrils, clung to her hair and permeated her clothes.

After she and Bryce had answered Perreth's questions for what seemed like hours, Bryce drove her to the hotel and insisted on accompanying her to her room. She should have objected. When he'd paused in the hallway, waiting for an invitation inside, she should have simply closed the door. But after what she'd seen at Sami's apartment, she couldn't bring herself to shut him out.

Sylvie listened to the rhythm of his footsteps as he paced the floor outside the bathroom door. She couldn't imagine what she would have done if she'd come across Sami's body by herself. Even now, the horror of it hung on the edges of her mind, as strong and hard to get rid of as the memory of that smell.

She leaned on the vanity. A sob worked up her throat and echoed in the bathroom. She could never forget how she'd felt walking into that apartment, smelling that odor and thinking in the back of her mind that it could be Diana. That her sister really might be dead.

A knock on the door. "Sylvie? Are you okay?"

She grasped the towel, pulling the terrycloth tighter around her body. "I'm fine."

"You sure?"

"Of course, I'm—" Her voice broke. She closed her eyes.

"Open the door."

Sylvie had to pull herself together. She couldn't hide in here and make him worry she was falling apart. "Just a second."

She let the towel fall to the floor and pulled on her robe. Tying the sash securely, she took a deep breath and opened the door. "See? I'm okay."

Bryce searched her eyes. "Sure?"

Barely above a whisper, his one word carried so much concern, tears came to her eyes.

She turned away.

"Sylvie." He met her gaze in the mirror. "You've never seen a dead body before, have you?"

They might not have known each other very long, but the events of the past few days had convinced her that at times he knew what she was feeling before she did. "I keep seeing his eyes."

"Don't think about it."

A sob hiccupped in her throat. "I keep seeing Diana."

He wrapped his arms around her. His chest and the firm plane of his stomach pressed against her back.

The press of his body felt so good, so right...

"I can't do this."

His breath whispered against her neck. "Just let me hold you."

A shiver rippled over her skin. Not a shiver of cold, though. A shiver of anticipation. She wanted him to hold her. She wanted much more. But... "You might be gone tomorrow."

"I won't be. I'll be right here."

"That's worse."

Bryce's eyebrows dipped low.

He deserved an explanation. As much as she didn't want to voice her fears, her insecurities, he deserved to know where he stood. "The longer you're here, the more I'll rely on you. The more I'll..."

Her voice faltered. *The more she'd what?*

"You're still worried I'll leave you in the lurch."

She nodded.

"I won't."

She wanted to believe him.

"You can trust me, Sylvie."

She swallowed into an aching throat. "I do trust you on some level. I just..."

"Can't go that far?"

"Cowardly, huh?"

"There's nothing about you that's cowardly." Slipping his hand along her cheek, he brushed her hair back from her face, draping it over her shoulder. "Just let me hold you. That's all. It doesn't have to go further than that."

His offer sounded good. It sounded wonderful. The trouble was, if she gave in, if she opened herself to temptation, *she* would be the one who wanted it to go further. *She* would be the one who needed more.

"Okay, okay. I don't want to pressure you. I'll rub your back. How about that?"

"I..."

"Or a foot massage. That's what you need. And let me tell you, I don't offer that to just anyone. Free of charge."

"I'm not sure how I can resist." Sylvie meant the remark to sound like a light quip, but she couldn't help feeling the truth of it. Bryce made her feel so warm, so wanted. As though she'd finally found her place in the world. A place where she belonged. A place she might even be able to pretend was permanent.

But permanent didn't exist. She knew that. So what if she didn't let herself think that way? What if she focused on only one night?

Could she do that?

She needed Bryce. No question. Needed his warmth and his passion. Needed to feel as if she belonged. If he was gone tomorrow, wouldn't she regret not being with him while she could? Wouldn't that be worse?

Sylvie turned in Bryce's arms. Tilting her head back, she peered up at him. "I'm sure you're great at foot massages, but I'm afraid I need more."

"A foot massage and a back rub?"

"More than that." She turned again to face the mirror, her back to him.

He watched her in the mirror, his eyes dark, intense, looking into her, waiting for what she'd do next.

Sylvie untied the sash at her waist. Fingers trembling, she

pulled the sides of her robe apart and slipped it off her shoulders. She stood naked in front of the mirror, in front of him. Her breasts hung free, her nipples puckered and taut. Warmth curled between her legs.

She felt his gaze move over her as much as she saw it in the mirror. His eyes took in every detail, as if every inch of her skin was precious, every feature unique, the whole package more alluring than any woman he'd ever seen. "You are so beautiful."

Sylvie let his gaze and words and the feelings building inside engulf her. If she had this man looking at her just this way every day, she'd feel beautiful the rest of her life.

She'd feel wanted.

She pushed away a shiver of fear. She couldn't think of anything right now but Bryce, the time they had together. She couldn't concentrate on anything but the reflection of his eyes.

He pressed his body close once again. The ridge of his erection jutted against her bottom and lower back. The crisp fabric of his shirt rubbed against her.

Slipping his arms around her, he cupped her breasts in his hands, lifting, caressing. Her nipples poked between his fingers. Lowering his mouth, he kissed her neck, her shoulder. He slid one hand down her side and over her belly until he found the heat between her legs.

Her belly tightened, low and hot. A moan vibrated deep in her throat, a sound she didn't even recognize as her own. She rocked against him, the heat building. But she wanted more.

Reaching behind her, she gripped his shirt and pulled it from his pants. She wanted to feel his skin, his warmth. She needed all of him. She didn't want him to hold anything back.

He took his hands from her, stripped off his clothing, and slipped on a condom. When he snuggled up behind her again, his skin smoothed warm against hers, his erection pressed against her, branding her with its heat. Nudging her legs apart, he moved closer, pushing between her thighs. But he didn't enter her. Instead he pressed tight against her. Taking a breast in each hand, he kissed her neck. He dipped his tip into her wetness.

Heat rippled through her, burgeoning with each stroke. She watched his hands lift her breasts, scissoring her nipples between his fingers. She felt the desire in his eyes, reveled in the hardness thrusting between her legs, rubbing, building. Pleasure shuddered through her and broke loose from her lips.

His strokes quickened, eliciting more shudders. Just when she thought she was done, he slipped inside. He filled her, stretched her, yet she felt no pain. Only slick heat.

She watched him move into her. His eyes were half closed, yet she could tell he was watching her, too. Watching her breasts bounce with each thrust. Watching the way she tilted her head back against him. Watching as the sounds of pleasure moaned deep in her throat.

Bryce leaned forward, his breath tickling her ear. "I can't get enough of you, Sylvie. I could never get enough."

She soaked in the words, the sensations. She couldn't get enough of him either. He was what she needed. What she'd always needed.

Slipping out of her, he scooped her into his arms and carried her out of the bathroom and laid her gently on the very edge of the bed. Nudging her legs apart, he settled between them and lowered his mouth to her.

She never guessed her body would still have the stamina

to respond. He moved his mouth over her, devouring her until waves of shudders seized her again.

She cried out, louder this time. She could no longer control her response. She could no longer control her feelings.

Pressure bore down on her chest, making it hard to breathe. It was too much, too fast, too dangerous, but she was falling for him anyway. Sometime tonight, she'd stepped over that cliff, and now she was plummeting.

Now she would never be the same.

Bryce

When Bryce awoke with sun peeking around the drapes and Sylvie curled at his side, he wasn't sure if he'd made a new start or a big mistake. Either way, he'd do it all over again in a heartbeat.

He watched her eyes move under her closed lids. Her hair spread over the pillow in wild waves. A smile played on her lips, the corners rising and falling with the flow of her dream. She looked peaceful. More peaceful than she had since he'd met her. And he could only hope that he was a part of that.

Sylvie hadn't wanted to admit it, but seeing Yamal dead had hit her hard, and Bryce knew that ever-present fear for her sister was no small part of it. He probably shouldn't have come back to her room, shouldn't have asked her to open the bathroom door, shouldn't have kissed her, but he hadn't been able to stop himself. He hadn't wanted to stop himself. Now he only hoped that she didn't regret making love. That she knew how much he really cared about her.

He glanced at the desk and the folder holding the articles about Ed Dryden that Diana had collected. Bryce hadn't shown them to Sylvie. He hadn't wanted her to know the role he'd played. Hadn't wanted to see the look in her eyes.

But after last night...

Bryce wanted to be honest. He wanted her to know him. And the only way for her to truly understand the man he had become was to know the man he once was.

He looked back to her sleeping face. So beautiful. So strong. So sweet. He bent over her and touched his lips to hers.

Her lids fluttered. Her eyes opened.

"Good morning."

At first, she looked confused. Then she gave him a tentative smile. "What time is it?"

"Just after seven."

She moved to sit up, clutching the sheet to shield her breasts. "I need to find out when the DNA test will—"

He held up a hand. "Wait."

She sucked in a breath and looked at him, as if suddenly remembering what had passed between them. Or maybe she was just finally acknowledging it.

Something inside him hesitated. The connection between them was so tender, so new, anything could destroy it, much less what he was about to confess. But if it was to grow, he had to be honest. He lowered his lips to hers again, kissing her for what might be the last time. "We have to talk."

"About what?" Her eyes darted, searching his.

"Last night was more than I'd ever dreamed."

She let out a breath of relief.

"What I have to tell you happened long before last night."

She frowned, a crease digging between her eyebrows. "What is it?"

"I never really told you..." He trailed off, searching for the words. How could he describe how single minded he'd been? How ambitious? "Why don't I show you?"

Throwing back the sheets, he thrust himself out of bed. Naked, he crossed the floor to the desk and picked up the folder.

The shrill ring of Sylvie's phone cut through the room.

Sylvie grabbed the phone and brought it to her ear. "Hello?"

Bryce sat on the bed next to her, the folder in his hands.

Tears pooled in the corners of Sylvie's eyes. "Bobby. I'm so glad to hear your voice. We'll be right there."

Diana

Diana didn't have to see him to sense he was back.

"Why are you doing this?" she asked.

No answer.

Why should she expect anything else?

She was no one.

Nothing.

"I didn't do this. He did."

The voice was so quiet that at first she wondered if she heard it at all. "He? Who?"

"You should have told me you found your sister."

"My sister?" A fresh wave of terror pumped into her bloodstream. "Sylvie?"

"Yes, Sylvie."

That voice… It was so familiar. Diana recognized that voice. "Do I know you?"

Sylvie

When Sylvie had heard Bobby's voice over the phone, she was so relieved she could hardly speak. Now that Bobby was awake, they'd find Diana for sure. Now that Bobby was awake, Perreth would have to keep them in the loop. Now that Bobby was awake, everything would be okay.

But seeing Bobby lying in the hospital bed—skin as white as the pillow his shaved head rested on, struggling for each molecule of oxygen from the tube threaded under his nose—she wasn't so sure.

Bryce hung back, leaning against the jamb, as if to give her space to talk to Bobby before she had to explain his presence. A consideration she appreciated.

Crossing to the bed, Sylvie realized they weren't alone. Giving the blond woman standing in the corner of the room a passing glance and nod, Sylvie stopped at Bobby's bedside and focused on him. "How are you feeling?"

The corner of his lips twitched in a smile. "Great."

At least he hadn't lost his sense of humor. She took his hand in hers, carefully skirting the IV needle, and gave him a teasing smile that she didn't feel. "I thought you were dead."

"If you hadn't found me so quickly, I might be."

"I wish I would have found you a lot quicker than I did."

"Why? So the bastard could have kidnapped you too?"

"So you know about Diana."

He glanced at the woman in the corner. "Yes."

Sylvie followed his gaze.

With thick blond hair and a face that could grace magazine covers, the woman should be beautiful. But there was something hard about her—a sharp glint in her eyes, a tension to her lips—something that made Sylvie a little uncomfortable.

"Sylvie, this is Valerie Ryker," Bobby said. "She's a consultant with the sheriff's department."

The woman stepped across the room and offered Sylvie her hand. "I'm sorry about your sister. I can assure you Detective Perreth and the local police are doing everything they can to find her."

Sylvie wasn't so sure about that, but she shook the woman's hand anyway. "Thank you... detective?"

"I'm a civilian consultant, not an officer. Not anymore. Call me Val."

"This is Bryce Walker. He's been helping me." It seemed like such a lame explanation, one that didn't even begin to describe their relationship. But then, Sylvie wasn't sure of their relationship herself, so how could she describe it to others?

Val narrowed her eyes on Bryce. "It's nice to meet you, counselor."

Bryce nodded but said nothing.

Bobby broke the silence. "Stan Perreth says you've been searching for Diana."

Sylvie focused on Bobby. If she was in his place, no matter how weak she was, she'd want to know what was going on. All of it. "Did Perreth tell you about the burned body they found?"

"That's part of what we need to talk to you about," Bobby said. "Perreth was just here. He got a call from the lab."

A cold sweat slicked Sylvie's back.

Bryce crossed the waxed tile and stopped beside her.

She knew why he'd moved closer. To be there for her if...

"It's not a match, Sylvie. It's not Diana."

Sylvie's knees sagged like rubber.

Bryce placed a hand on her elbow, steadying her.

She gave him a grateful glance. She could handle this. If Diana was still alive, Sylvie could handle anything.

"There's more," Val said.

Sylvie's mood plummeted back into worry, as if riding a roller coaster.

Bobby leaned his head back on his pillow. If possible, he looked worse than he had when they'd arrived.

"Ten days ago, the body of a woman was found up near Lake Loyal," Val said.

Sylvie nodded. "I remember hearing something about that."

"What you didn't hear was that the body found Saturday in Madison that Perreth thought might be Diana had certain characteristics in common with that first victim near Lake Loyal."

"What characteristics?" Bryce asked.

"Both victims were women, obviously. Both were killed with a knife. And there were other similarities, things I am not going to get into."

Sylvie thought of the reasons Perreth had given for not letting her see the body. "Something was done to them that made them unrecognizable?"

"That's where the second body differed. But virtually everything else matches. And the other elements of this killer's signature are very distinctive."

"Signature?" Sylvie had skimmed enough articles about Ed Dryden to know what that word signified. "Are you talking about a serial killer here?"

"It's possible."

For a civilian, Val sure gave answers that were as vague as any cop's. The familiar hum grew louder in Sylvie's ears. "Why are you telling us any of this?"

"Whoever killed these two women has a signature that is very close to a killer who struck Wisconsin a number of years ago."

His name stuck in Sylvie's throat.

"Ed Dryden," Bryce supplied.

Val stared at Bryce a good long while, then nodded.

"But he's in prison." Sylvie's voice barely rose above a whisper. The image of Diana running through the forest lodged in her mind. Diana being hunted like an animal, the way Ed Dryden had done with most of his victims. "How could he do this if he's in prison? Is he in prison?"

"This isn't Ed Dryden himself. He's still at Bainsbridge. But whoever this is seems to be copying his signature nearly exactly."

Sylvie's mind jumped ahead—to why the lieutenant was telling her this, to what it had to do with her. With Diana. "They're blond, aren't they? The two women?"

"Yes."

"And they look like Dryden's original victims?"

"As far as we can tell. Yes."

She thought of the scenario she and Bryce had discussed. "Do you think Dryden is controlling this copycat? Controlling him from his prison cell?"

"I suppose it could be possible. If he was communicating with someone on the outside." Again Val's gaze drilled into Bryce. "The copycat is reproducing details about Dryden's murders that only someone privy to the case files would know."

"Like a detective." Sylvie glanced at Bryce.

"Or someone who devoted his life to studying Dryden," Bryce countered.

Suddenly Sylvie knew why Val was telling her about

these murders. "Diana. You're afraid that Diana will be the third."

Bryce placed his palm gently on her back.

Regaining her balance, Sylvie swung her focus to Bobby. "Do you know about the research project? The interviews Diana was doing with Ed Dryden?"

"Perreth filled me in this morning."

"Diana didn't tell you?"

"No."

So Diana had kept her fascination with Dryden secret from Bobby too.

Why?

"Perreth has talked to Professor Bertram about Diana's involvement in his research," Val said. "Unfortunately, he never got a chance to interview Bertram's assistant. And as I understand it, the two of you found his body last night."

Sylvie nodded. The last thing she wanted to do was relive that moment. But if it would help, she was all in. "Detective Perreth said it looked like suicide."

"And you don't believe that?" Bobby asked.

"I don't know what to believe. I suppose it's possible."

"Perreth seems to think there's a chance Sami Yamal was the copycat killer. That it got to be too much for him, and that's why he took his own life. Do you think that's possible?" Val Ryker looked at her, and then turned those laser eyes to Bryce once again.

"I don't know," Sylvie said finally. "We only talked to him once. But he insisted he was the real expert on Dryden. He resented the professor's book deal and that Diana was working with him."

"If Yamal was the copycat, it's over." Bobby said.

Sylvie frowned. "I suppose it would be."

"I mean, it could really be all over, Sylvie. If he took Diana, we might never find her."

Sylvie's chest felt tight. She strained to breathe.

No, no, no...

"Wait. Wait."

All eyes focused on Sylvie.

"You have considered that Dryden could be behind this, right?"

"Behind it?" Val parroted.

"You know, pulling the strings? Didn't you just suggest that?"

"No, you did."

Sylvie nodded. "Right, right... and it could be possible."

Val glanced at Bryce. "It could be. All we know for certain is that the killer knows details the general public doesn't."

Bryce slipped an arm around Sylvie. His body pressed against her side, solid, close. But she couldn't take comfort in his presence this time. She couldn't take comfort in anything.

She'd been so naive through all this. Purposefully so. She'd stubbornly clung to the hope that she'd be able to find Diana. That Bryce could help her get the answers she needed. That once Bobby regained consciousness the three of them could work together to get her sister back. But the truth was, an entire law firm of Bryces and a whole department of Bobbys and Val Rykers couldn't find Diana before it was too late.

But Sylvie might just have a shot.

She pulled away from Bryce's side. Forcing steel into her spine, she focused on Val. "I want you to set up a meeting for me."

"A meeting with who?"

"I'm going to talk to Ed Dryden."

Bryce

Sylvie's words crashed down on Bryce's skull with the force of a sledgehammer. She couldn't be suggesting what she was suggesting. "You're not meeting with him."

Sylvie balled her hands into fists by her sides, as if readying for a knock-down drag-out. "It's not your choice to make."

"It might not be, but that doesn't mean it's one *you* should make. He's dangerous. You can't walk into that prison and have a chat with a monster like that. It's like waving a red flag in front of a rabid bull."

"Even if the copycat isn't Sami Yamal, he already knows I'm Diana's sister. He's already tried to kidnap me. I'm already a target. Talking to Dryden isn't going to make any difference."

"What do you think Dryden is going to do? Tell you where Diana is? Call off his copycat?"

"I might learn something from him. Something that could help."

Bryce couldn't believe his ears. He looked to Bobby. "You can't let her do this."

"Sylvie, I'm afraid Bryce is right," Bobby said.

Sylvie kept her eyes on Bryce. "Why are you acting like I'm not in danger already? You were there. If you hadn't gotten me out of that van, I'd be with the copycat right now. I have nothing to lose."

"You have your life to lose," Bryce said.

"You're not listening to me."

"You're right. I'm not listening. And if listening means thinking what you're proposing is a good idea, I'll sure as hell *never* listen." He glared at Bobby. "You have to tell her to forget it."

"He's right, Sylvie," Bobby said again.

Bryce turned to Val Ryker. She was already staring at him, as she had since they'd walked in the door... since she'd called him counselor without anyone having mentioned he was an attorney. "Sylvie can't do this. You can't let her do this."

"I'm not in charge here."

She could have fooled him. With Bobby still in bad shape, Val Ryker seemed to be manipulating the entire conversation, throwing comments out there and watching how the rest of them reacted.

Especially him.

As if she knew he was Dryden's attorney. As if she knew all of it.

"I'd like to hear your opinion," Bryce told her. "Meeting with Dryden will put Sylvie at risk. You can't think this is a good idea."

Val hesitated, as if coming up with her next move. "I've never been face-to-face with Ed Dryden, but I have had an experience with a man who was somewhat similar. You don't want to let someone like that into your life. He'll only cause you pain."

Sylvie's eyes glistened. She shook her head. "That's just it. Diana's my twin. My only family. If he has anything to do with what happened to her, he's already in my life. I need help getting him out. Will you help me? Please?"

Val Ryker considered this for a moment. "He's a manipulator. You'll have to assume every word out of his mouth is a lie."

Sylvie nodded.

"I want to observe the meeting, bring in an expert if I can," Val continued. "And we'll need to record it."

Sylvie nodded again.

Bryce looked from one woman to the other. "What just happened? Have you both gone crazy? This man is dangerous."

Sylvie glanced up at him, her chin jutting slightly. "He's in prison. He won't be able to hurt me."

"Not unless there's someone on the outside, as you pointed out before." Val again, her eyes drilling into Bryce. "Someone who is communicating with him."

Bryce's throat felt thick, hot. If only he'd made time to talk to Sylvie this morning, tell her everything. Maybe he could have prevented this idea from even popping into her head. But *if onlys* only got him so far. "I need to talk to you, Sylvie."

"We *are* talking."

"Alone. Now."

"I'm not going to change my mind, Bryce."

"Just hear me out. Give me that much."

She glanced at Bobby and Val. Finally, Sylvie nodded.

Bryce led her out of the room. Privacy. They needed someplace private. He didn't want the whole hospital to hear what he was about to say.

Weaving through a maze of hallways, he negotiated his way to the rooftop deck. Sun sparkled off the two main lakes and bathed the narrow isthmus of buildings stretching between. Not far away, the capitol dome caught the sun. The golden statue on its pinnacle stabbed into a blue sky. Pleasant, if not for the cold current of wind. Wind that chilled him to the bone.

Leaning against the rail, Sylvie wrapped her arms around herself. She squinted up at him. "Okay. Talk."

He shrugged out of his coat and attempted to drape it over her shoulders.

She held up a hand. "I don't need your coat. I need to hear what you have to say. What you couldn't say inside."

"I wanted to tell you this morning, when you woke up." He draped his coat over the rail. His chest ached with each breath. His throat pinched, the words he had to say strangling him. But he had to get them out. He had no pictures, no articles to explain it for him this time. "Yesterday you asked about Dryden's lawyer."

Her eyebrows pulled together. "What about him?"

"I *am* Dryden's lawyer, Sylvie. Or at least, I was until about six weeks ago."

She didn't move, didn't gasp, nothing. She just stared at him with steady eyes, waiting for him to explain.

"When the lawsuits against the Supermax prison started a few years ago, I decided to get in on it. Thought it would give the law firm some press, bring in more clients."

"But Dryden? Why Dryden?"

"Because he would bring the big headlines." The picture he was painting for her made him feel sick, but he couldn't stop. It was the truth. He had been that man, chasing notoriety, playing with the law like it was a game. So wrapped up in his own greed and ambition that he couldn't see anything else.

"And this is what you wanted to tell me?"

"No. I mean, yes, but it's not everything."

She hugged herself tighter. "What else?"

"I won the suit against the Supermax. I got Dryden transferred to another facility. One with less restrictive conditions, less solitary confinement. But that wasn't enough for him."

"What did he want?"

Bryce looked out at the skyline, at the blue curves of the lakes. He'd gotten Dryden nearly everything he'd asked for, everything the monster didn't deserve. "He wasn't happy with Banesbridge. Most of the prison has been renovated since he escaped in 1996. And what wasn't is under renovation now. Security has been improved."

"And he wanted someplace less secure."

Bryce nodded. He remembered the grin on Dryden's thin lips when he'd made his demand clear. "When I refused to go along, he threatened me."

"What did you do?"

"Nothing." And he'd never forgive himself for it. "I underestimated him. He was in prison. He couldn't get out. He couldn't hurt me from behind bars."

Sylvie's throat moved under tender skin, as if she was struggling to swallow all he'd told her, trying to prepare for what came next. "Your brother..."

"The whole thing was my damn fault." He waited for that look he dreaded. One of disgust. Horror. Condemnation. The one he'd seen in the mirror every morning for the past six weeks.

It never came. Instead she stepped close and put her arms around him. "I'm sorry, Bryce. I'm so sorry."

Pain pressed behind his eyes and knifed through his sinuses. He'd expected a lot of things, but not this. As much as he thought of Sylvie, as much as he cared about her, he'd underestimated her.

He loved her.

And now... now that he'd found her, he was on the brink of losing her. "Don't do this, Sylvie. Please. Promise you'll stay away from him."

Tears spiked her lashes and trickled down her cheeks. "I know how awful this must be for you, Bryce. I understand now."

His throat closed. He knew where she was leading before she said the words. He knew her decision would scar her forever. And if he lost her because of it, it would destroy him.

"But I need you to understand me, too."

Sylvie

Sylvie shifted in her chair. Crossing and uncrossing her legs, she finally settled on crossing her ankles, knees pressed tightly together.

She'd never been inside the walls of a prison before. And even though she was in the main building, far from the cell blocks, she already knew she never wanted to come to a place like this again. She didn't mind the Spartan room, furnished with only a scarred table and four chairs, one bolted to the floor. She didn't mind the antiseptic smell. She didn't even mind the dour-faced guards.

What she hated was the sound of doors locking behind them as they passed through the sally ports. And that no matter how deeply she inhaled, she couldn't seem to breathe.

She glanced at the camera in the corner of the room. Bryce was watching through that camera, along with Val Ryker, Detective Perreth, Professor Bertram, and others Sylvie didn't know. Bryce had insisted on coming with her, a demand that made her want to cry. She knew this was hell for him, seeing the man he thought responsible for killing his brother. The fact that he'd stuck by her, even through this, made her heart squeeze. She only hoped it wasn't all in vain, that she could coax something of value from Ed Dryden, something that would lead to finding Diana.

The door opened. Two uniformed guards stepped into the

room, and between them, hands and feet shackled, shuffled Ed Dryden.

He looked much like his photograph, only older. Brown hair now silver, he appeared as if he should be wearing a nice suit or a relaxed weekend baseball shirt, not the baggy prison jumpsuit. Although he was clearly in his fifties, the boyish quality she'd noticed in his photograph was still there. The slightly weak slant to his chin, the disarming arch to his eyebrows—all of it conspired to make him appear more like the nice next-door neighbor than an infamous killer. He raised his eyes to hers.

His eyes were like his picture too. Ice blue. And void of emotion.

She suppressed a shiver.

The corners of thin lips lifted in a smile. "Sylvie. You're as beautiful as your sister."

"I want to talk to you about Diana," Sylvie said in a thankfully steady voice.

So far, so good.

He lowered himself into the chair.

The guards handcuffed his hands to the steel rails. One gave her a pointed look. "Are you sure you don't want one of us to stay in here with you?"

Of course, she did. Better yet, she wanted Bryce and everyone else in here as well, not merely watching from the next room. "I'll be fine."

"Of course you will be," Dryden said, voice low and melodic. "I'm no animal, despite what they imply with their handcuffs and chains. I'm well read, civilized. I know how to treat a lady."

Sylvie resisted the urge to look at the camera. Only she could do this now. And no one could help her.

She folded her hands in her lap, picking at her fingernails. "I'm not sure how to ask this."

"I've found the direct approach is best."

Right. And she'd be willing to bet Dryden was as direct as a crazy straw. "I'm glad you feel that way."

He smiled, thin lips pulling back to reveal straight white teeth. She caught a whiff of mint mouthwash, as if he'd gargled just for her.

"My sister has disappeared."

His smile faded. "When?"

"Saturday afternoon. Someone kidnapped her from her wedding. Do you know where she is?"

His eyebrows dipped low. A muscle twitched in his clean-shaven cheek. "Why would you think I know anything? If you haven't noticed, I don't get out much."

"That wasn't a very direct answer."

"Forgive me. I'm a bit shaken by the news."

He looked about as shaken as a professional poker player. "I'm worried about Diana. I've come here for your help."

"My help." A smile curved the corners of his lips.

"Yes."

"That is as it should be, isn't it?"

As it should be?

Clearly he liked the position of power that her coming to him for help gave him. Power over her. But although the thought of giving this man any kind of power over her turned her stomach, she would do whatever it took to find Diana. "Will you help me find my sister?"

He leaned back in his chair. "I'm sorry I have to let you down, Sylvie. But I don't know where your sister is."

"Please. You're a powerful man. I know you're in touch with someone outside of prison."

"Why would you think that?"

"I... I just do."

"And you think I asked someone to take Diana?"

"Did you?"

Closing his eyes, he shook his head. "I expected more from you."

She wouldn't let him throw her off track. "Please answer my question."

"I didn't have anything to do with your sister's disappearance. I have no reason to want to hurt her."

Too bad she didn't believe him. "Two women have been murdered recently."

He lifted an eyebrow in surprise.

The gesture felt forced. "They were killed in the same way you killed your victims. The same exact way."

"And what way is that?"

Did he want her to describe the murders? To voice the horrible things he'd done? The thought made her sick. "I don't think you need me to tell you what you already know."

"No. But I do need you to tell me why you think Diana is among these women. That's why you're here, right? You think Diana is the third? Or you're afraid she will be?"

"Is she?"

"I don't know anything about these women you speak of, but I can assure you that I have no reason to hurt your sister."

Except that Diana looked like the wife he murdered.

"You don't look convinced."

"I've seen pictures of the women you killed. Pictures of your wife. Diana looks just like her."

"Yes, Adrianna." A gleam lit his eyes that made Sylvie want to bolt for the door. "Diana does look like her. Of course, you do too."

She swallowed and forced herself to meet those cold eyes. "These other women are blond too."

"Oh?" Another raise of the eyebrows in feigned surprise.

Maybe Bryce was right. Maybe she'd been stupid to think she'd get any answers from Ed Dryden. Maybe the smart thing would be for her to walk out that door and forget she'd ever laid eyes on the serial killer. But she couldn't do that. She had to give it one last try. "Help me find Diana. Please, Mr. Dryden."

He narrowed his eyes. "Hmm. That's not right."

"Not right? What isn't right?"

"You calling me *Mr. Dryden*. I don't like it."

She'd call him babycakes if that was what it took to win his cooperation. "What would you like me to call you? Ed?"

He shook his head. "That's not right, either."

"Eddie?"

"No, no, no..."

Frustration knotted in her gut, replacing the edgy feeling of nausea. She wished she could be cool, detached, beat him at his own game, but she couldn't. She needed him. "Please, where is Diana?"

"I told you, I don't know where she is. I wish I did. Believe me, I'm as worried about her as you are."

She ground her teeth together. She was getting mighty tired of his false charm. She felt like spitting in his face. "I can tell you're eaten up."

"Sylvie, Sylvie, there's no reason for sarcasm." He shook his head as if he was disappointed in her again. "I can tell you what I know about your sister. Maybe that will help you see that I mean what I say."

Maybe Bryce was right. Maybe he wasn't going to tell her anything of value. He was just playing her again. Nonetheless, she found herself leaning forward in her chair. "What do you know?"

"I know she's beautiful, like you. She's smart, like you. But that isn't surprising, is it? Not with identical twins." He leaned back in his chair and looked past her at the wall, as if lost in private thoughts.

Sylvie clasped her hands together to keep them from shaking. What was he thinking about? Times during Diana's interviews with him when he manipulated her like he was trying to manipulate Sylvie? Or was he fantasizing about the hell Diana was going through now?

"Diana had this puppet she liked to play with. A Mexican clown. She loved that thing. She never let it out of her sight. It was her favorite, along with the music box. You both loved the music box."

Sylvie narrowed her eyes on Dryden. Had he lost his mind? Slipped into some kind of delusional fantasy world? The articles she'd read about Dryden stated that he wasn't insane, but if this rambling wasn't insanity, what was it? "Excuse me?"

"You, of course, were too sick for puppets." He shifted his stare back to her. "I'm glad to see you so strong. You turned out as beautiful and strong as your sister."

Her mind stuttered. She struggled to grasp what he was saying. "I don't understand."

"Of course, you don't. You were too young. Young but sweet. You used to look up to me like I was a god. You made me feel like a god. That's when I realized things were all wrong. That I had to change my life. I had to take control. Be what I was meant to be."

Her throat constricted, making it hard to swallow, hard to

speak. "I'm sorry, Mr. Dryden. I don't know what you're talking about."

"Didn't I tell you I don't want you calling me Mr. Dryden?"

"I'm sorry."

He shifted in his chair, chains rattling. His eyes glinted like glittering ice. "Do you know what I want you to call me, Sylvie? Have you figured it out yet?"

"What?" Her voice was only a whisper, but suddenly she wished she could take the word back. She wished she could jump from her chair and race out of the room. She wished she'd never set foot in this prison, never heard of Ed Dryden.

But as much as she wanted to change the past, she couldn't. Nor could she alter what would happen next. She waited for him to tell her the name, feeling as powerless to stop him as a three-year-old.

His thin lips spread into a slow smile. "Daddy. I want you to call me Daddy."

Bryce

Bryce threw the door open and pushed into the prison's interview room. He had to get Sylvie out of here. Away from this monster. Dryden had gone too far. Much too far. "This meeting is over."

Val Ryker and Stan Perreth stepped into the room behind him along with two guards.

Sylvie didn't look up. She didn't move. She just stared at her hands, as if she didn't hear him, as if she didn't know any of them were there. She picked compulsively at her fingernails.

"Hello, counselor."

Bryce kept his eyes on Sylvie and off Dryden. One look at

that smirk and Bryce wasn't sure he could prevent himself from choking the life out of him.

"All right, Dryden," one of the guards said in a bored voice. "Your fun is done for the day. Time to go back to your cell."

The other guard glanced at Bryce, Sylvie, and the officers. "If the rest of you don't mind leaving first..."

Val nodded. "Thank you."

"Sylvie?" Bryce said in a gentle voice.

Sylvie didn't look up.

He knelt beside her and grasped her hands, stopping the frantic clawing movement of her fingers. "Sylvie?"

She moved her gaze to his face, but he couldn't sense any kind of a connection looking into her eyes. She seemed to be staring through him at another world. A world very far away.

She must be in shock. Why the hell wouldn't she be? He sure was. He didn't know what to think, what to feel, what to believe. Astonishment, denial, and anger tangled inside him like a writhing snake. But he couldn't sort it out now. He had to focus, to keep himself together until after he got Sylvie far away from Ed Dryden.

"Let's get out of here, Sylvie. Come on." Gently Bryce pulled her up out of her chair.

"Think twice before trusting a lawyer, Sylvie. Especially this one." Dryden's voice prodded him like a blunt stick poking at a wounded animal. "He's the type that will use you to further his own agenda. A truly manipulative and selfish breed."

Bryce ground his teeth until his jaw hurt. "If I were you, Dryden, I'd shut the hell up. You're an awfully stationary target."

"What kind of a daddy would I be if I didn't offer my little girl some fatherly advice?"

Bryce's pulse pounded in his ears, pushing him closer to the edge.

Dryden couldn't be Sylvie's father. Bryce wouldn't believe it. And if that bastard didn't shut up, Bryce would put his hands on either side of his head and snap his neck like a twig. Make him pay for all he'd done. The idea of it was so sweet, it was all Bryce could do to force his feet to move toward the door. "Come on, Sylvie. Don't listen to him. He's just trying to hurt you."

"I would never hurt Sylvie. She's my daughter, Walker. My little girl."

No. No. No.

Sylvie stopped, she turned to face Dryden. "My mother. She was your wife?"

"We could have been the perfect little family. But unlike you and your sister, she didn't understand me. She never did."

Bryce angled his body between Dryden and Sylvie. He pulled her toward the door.

She hesitated.

"Come on, Sylvie."

"Maybe she doesn't want to go with you, Walker. Maybe she wants to stay and talk. She hasn't seen her daddy in more than twenty years."

"Go to hell, Dryden."

"Eventually. And when I get there, I'll be sure to say hello to Tanner for you."

Bryce let go of Sylvie's hand. Dodging around the cops, he launched himself at Dryden and slammed a fist into the bastard's nose.

Cartilage gave under Bryce's knuckles. Dryden's head snapped back. A spray of blood misted the air, hot and sticky.

Hands clawed at Bryce, grabbing him, pinning his arms behind his back. Val and Perreth dragged Bryce away.

"I wish I could let you at him," Perreth said, dipping his lips close to Bryce's ear. "You'd be doing the world a favor."

Once the cops dragged Bryce clear of the room, they released his arms.

"Stay here," Val Ryker said to Bryce. She focused on Sylvie. "Remember what I said. Every word a lie."

Ryker and Perreth stepped back into the interview room and closed the door behind them.

Sylvie stared at the floor, tears brimming in her eyes.

Bryce clenched his hands into fists. His head throbbed. His mouth tasted of blood. How could Ed Dryden be Sylvie's father? How did any of this make sense?

It didn't.

"See? He was lying. Just like Val said."

Sylvie shook her head.

"He was manipulating you."

"He's telling the truth, Bryce."

"Don't be ridiculous."

"He knew... he knew about my heart."

"Diana could have told him."

"And that's why Diana visited him, why she was so interested..."

"You don't know that."

"But I do. Diana would never be a serial killer groupie. He's our—"

"Stop."

Sylvie shook her head. "And our mother... Diana and I, we look just like Adrianna Dryden. Just like her."

Her quiet words hit Bryce square in the sternum. He hadn't wanted to see it. He didn't want to acknowledge it now.

"He's my... my..." Sylvie looked up at Bryce.

Sylvie needed his help. He could see it in her eyes. In their desperate shine behind squinting lashes. She needed his help to sort through the shock, to understand what had just happened, to figure out what it meant.

Pressure built in his head. He groped inside himself. For something to give her, a word, a touch. But all that was there was the empty echo of Tanner's laugh. The scent of blood. And the smug look in Ed Dryden's eyes.

Bryce had to get out of here. Away from Dryden. Away from his regrets.

And—God forgive him—away from Sylvie.

Ed Dryden's daughter.

"I'm sorry, Sylvie. I... I'm just sorry." Bryce turned away from her and strode for the sally port and the hall beyond, leaving her all alone.

Sylvie

"I told Bryce to stay here." Val Ryker paced the floor of the narrow observation room, clearly angry.

Sylvie wrapped her arms around herself. She wished she could sink into her chair and disappear. Her chest ached. Still her lungs refused to fill with air. And no matter how many short gasps she took, she couldn't get the oxygen she needed.

Detective Perreth grunted. "Looks like we know who's carrying Dryden's messages."

Sylvie glanced from Perreth to Val. "You're not thinking Bryce..."

"He's the only one we don't have an eye on, and the punch could just be a cover," Perreth said. "You tell me."

"It's not Bryce."

Val watched her for a long while before she spoke. "Did you know he was Dryden's lawyer?"

Sylvie nodded. She could still hear the pain in Bryce's voice when he'd told her. The self-recrimination. The regret. "He hates Dryden. More than anything. He blames Dryden for killing his brother."

"The hunting accident?" Val asked. "Interesting."

Perreth started for the door. "Seems to me, he's been playing everybody. I'm going to have him picked up."

"Wait," Sylvie said, but he was gone.

"Bryce will have to answer for himself." Val put a hand on her arm. "Let's get you back to your hotel."

Sylvie didn't want to go back there. Where she'd given herself to Bryce. Where she'd thought she was in love. But she had nowhere else to go. "Okay."

Val escorted Sylvie out through the sally ports and helped her sign out. Outside, two police officers stopped talking as she emerged. Professor Bertram leaned on a police cruiser, puffing on a cigarette as if his life depended on it. He looked at Sylvie with bloodshot eyes. "I'm sorry he's your father. I wish it wasn't true."

Sylvie nodded. She didn't want to think about Dryden, but even now, she realized she could never escape him. He was part of her past. Part of her DNA. Every time she looked in the mirror, she'd now see his eyes. Every time she witnessed a father laughing with his daughter, she'd now hear his voice.

Daddy. I want you to call me Daddy.

Sylvie shuddered.

When Ed Dryden had told her that he was her father, she'd thought she'd hit bottom, but she'd been wrong. She hadn't known what bottom was until Bryce had walked away because of it. Because of who she was.

Val opened the front door of the police cruiser and motioned Sylvie inside. One of the two chatting officers slid into the driver's seat.

"You're not coming with me?" Sylvie asked Val.

"You need police protection, Sylvie."

Sylvie had forgotten Val was no longer a cop. Here she hadn't even known this woman yesterday, and yet she felt like the only connection Sylvie had left. And now she was losing even that...

"Everything will be okay," the officer said. "Name is Timms. I'll take good care of you."

Sylvie felt herself nod. She appreciated the reassurance. She really did. But everything wouldn't be okay. It would never be okay again.

Val said her goodbyes and walked over to talk to the professor. Officer Timms started the car, pulled out of the prison gate, and they were on their way.

Sylvie leaned back in the passenger seat of the police cruiser and struggled to catch her breath. She'd hoped once she emerged from behind the tall fences topped with curls of razor wire, she would be able to breathe.

No such luck.

At least Officer Timms turned out to be more of a talker than a listener and for that, Sylvie was grateful. He launched into a story about dogs giving birth and children mispronouncing words, the calm in his voice something she could cling to.

Sylvie wrapped her arms around herself. Gripping her

sweater's chunky knit with both hands, she watched the bluffs roll by, tree-covered swells, rock-strewn valleys, farm fields stretching in the distance.

A strange pulsing thump broke through her thoughts.

The sound grew louder. The patrol care started to buck.

"Damn it." The officer pulled to the shoulder and stopped.

"What happened?" Sylvie asked.

"Flat tire. Just you wait here. I'll have it fixed in a second." Officer Timms reported the problem on his radio then climbed out and circled to the back of the car.

Sylvie stared straight ahead, the setting sun highlighting every dead bug and water spot on the windshield. She wished she could cry, let the tears wash away the memories, the betrayals, the feelings she'd conjured out of loneliness and longing, but her eyes remained dry. She didn't have enough tears left. She would never have enough tears.

Another vehicle came around the curve in the road. Sylvie angled the rearview mirror just in time to see a light bar fire to life, flashing red and blue. It parked behind them. The driver's door opened, and the officer Timms had been talking to at the prison joined him.

The passenger door opened, and the professor got out.

One of the officers waved him away. "We got this. Stay in the car."

The professor returned to the car, but instead of climbing back inside, he paused for a moment and then walked back to the officers.

He bent down alongside them, all three studying the tire.

Sylvie went back to staring at the sunset, now almost gone behind the trees.

Shouts erupted from the back of the car.

"Hey! What are y—"

"Fu—"

Pop!

Pop!

Pop!

Sylvie couldn't move. Couldn't think. She could see nothing but shadows in the mirror, someone slumped against the car's trunk. Motion in the falling darkness.

Run!

Sylvie clawed at the door handle. Catching it on the third try, she shoved the door open and scrambled out.

An arm crashed down on her shoulder.

Her legs buckled, sending her sprawling.

A hand clamped her wrist, pulled her arm behind her back, and drove her face into the pavement.

Bryce

Bryce stood on the sidewalk, staring at Sylvie's hotel and the three police cars parked outside.

Hours of driving along curving highways and over rolling hills hadn't done a damn thing to clear his mind, but it had given him the chance to cool off, to shake the shock out of his system, and recognize what a dumbass he'd been.

Ed Dryden was a monster, no doubt. But Dryden couldn't destroy what Bryce had found with Sylvie. Of course, he didn't have to. By walking out on her just when she needed him most, Bryce had accomplished that all on his own.

So he'd driven to her hotel, ready to explain, to apologize, to throw himself down on his knees and beg her to forgive him. He'd assumed she'd have some kind of protection, but three cars seemed like a lot. He hoped they could get a moment alone.

Bryce opted to take the stairs instead of the elevator, using the extra time to rehearse the epic apology he'd put together on the way over. Reaching Sylvie's floor, he bounded out into the hall and came to a dead stop.

The hallway was full of cops.

Sylvie?

Heart beating double time, he made it as far as the hallway before a young uniformed cop stopped him.

"Whoa, whoa, whoa! No one's allowed beyond this point."

Bryce could see the door of Sylvie's room. It was open. Perreth's blue coat and bulldog jowls were visible just inside.

Visions of Sylvie bloodied and dead flashed in his mind. He shut the images out. He wouldn't think that way. He couldn't. He focused on the officer barring his way. "I need to talk to someone in charge."

"I'm sorry, sir. The detective is very busy. Leave your contact information with me, and I'll make sure he gets it."

"I have information that might help."

The officer looked at him sideways, as if he sensed a lie. "If you leave your phone number—"

"Listen, I'm an attorney. The woman under police protection, she's my client." *His client.* Funny, but Sylvie had never been his client, not officially.

But she was so much more.

"I told you to stay put," a woman's voice said from down the hall.

Bryce looked past the uniform and focused on Val Ryker, headed his way. Perreth peeked out of Sylvie's room then fell in behind her.

"Where in the hell did you go, Bryce?" she said.

"Out. Driving. Where's Sylvie?" Bryce pushed through, heading for the room.

"She's not here."

"Where is she?"

"She and Professor Bertram…" Val glanced at Perreth, as if passing the question to him.

"They were kidnapped. The officers protecting them shot."

Bryce watched Perreth's mouth form the words, but it still took a few more seconds for what he was saying to sink in.

Sylvie was gone.

"GPS led to the missing patrol car," Val said. "It's being pulled out of Lake Loyal now."

"I'm willing to bet the dash cam caught what happened," Perreth said, staring at Bryce. "If you're helping Dryden, if you did… all this. You might as well admit it now. Things will be easier for you."

Bryce's head pounded. "You can't really think I'm helping Dryden."

"You tell me."

Sylvie was—

Bryce shook the thought away. There was something that wasn't right here. Something that didn't add up. "It wasn't Dryden's copycat."

As soon as he heard his own words out loud, he knew his hunch was right. "It wasn't Dryden at all."

Ryker fixed him with an intense stare. "Why?"

"Sylvie and Diana… They're his daughters."

Perreth arched one brow. "So? You're not trying to tell us he loves them or something, are you?"

"Not in a million years, but Dryden does things for reasons. His own twisted reasons, but still. He wasn't angry with Sylvie. He wanted to charm her. Manipulate her. Why would he order some lackey to kidnap and kill either Sylvie or Diana as if they mean nothing?"

"That's not what Bertram thought." Perreth countered. "And he's studied the killer for years. He knows all about Dryden."

He knows all about Dryden.

The thought hit Bryce with the force of a kick.

Wouldn't an expert know Dryden had three-year-old twin daughters at the time that he killed his wife? And wasn't it possible he found out who those daughters were?

Bryce's heart beat high in his chest. The professor seemed to have pulled himself together at the prison. But just the day before he'd been a mess, upset and on the verge of tears. Could years of obsession with his daughter's murderer have taken their toll? Was it possible he'd decided to take from Dryden what Dryden had stolen from him?

God knew Dryden had gotten to Bryce. He'd forgotten everything but his hatred. He'd turned his back on his own happiness. He'd walked out on Sylvie when she'd needed him most.

"There's a letter," Bryce blurted out. "It was sent to Diana. I smuggled it out of her apartment the day she disappeared."

A low growl came from Perreth's throat.

"We assumed it was from Dryden, but..."

Val nodded. "You think it was from... who? Bertram?"

"Where is it?" Perreth barked.

"In her room. In the safe."

Sylvie

Sylvie's head throbbed. Her mouth felt dry and gritty as sand. She lay on her back in some sort of bed. A musty pillow supported her head, but she couldn't move her hands and feet, as if she was tied to the bed by wrists and ankles.

Through her lashes she could see outlines of windows where feeble light leeched around the edges of room-darkening shades. She willed her eyes to open, to adjust to the lack of light. But in the end of the room where she was tied, blackness still surrounded her, smothered her, beat her down.

"Sylvie? Are you awake?"

The voice was weak but familiar. A voice she had dreamed of hearing. A voice she was searching for. "Diana?"

"Sylvie. Over here."

Slowly she turned her aching head in the direction of Diana's voice. She couldn't see her sister's face. But the white glow of her wedding gown filtered through the dark.

"Diana. Thank God."

"Oh, Syl. I'm so sorry he got you too. I'm so sorry."

She tried to shake her head, pain erupting behind her eyes and shooting down the back of her neck. "Why would he do this, Diana?"

"There's a lot I haven't told you, Syl. So much you don't know."

"I saw Ed Dryden today."

"Then you *do* know." Diana's voice trembled. With shame. With regret.

Emotions Sylvie knew all too well. Emotions that clung to her skin, flowed through her blood and burrowed into the marrow of her bones. "Why didn't you tell me?"

A muffled sob rose in the darkness. The rustle of satin. "I didn't know what you'd do."

"What do you mean?"

"You were always so guarded. So aloof. Like you didn't trust me. I thought if I told you before we got to know each other, before we really felt like sisters, you wouldn't want anything to do with it. With me. That I'd never hear from you again."

Sylvie wanted to tell Diana she was wrong. That she never would have shied away from her sister no matter how ugly reality was. But the truth was, she didn't know how she would have reacted.

Sylvie took in a deep breath of musty-smelling air.

She might not know how she would have felt six months ago, but she knew how she felt now. "He's my father too, Diana. And as much as I want to run from that, I'd never run from you."

"I'm so sorry, Syl."

"It's okay."

"No, it's not. I'm weak, Sylvie. I've always been weak, and some people... they can just sense it."

"That's not your fault."

"Maybe not at first. But now... Look where I am. The same spot I've been trying to escape my whole life. And because of me, now you're here too."

Sylvie focused on the glow of her sister's gown, the gleam of her blond hair. Diana was the strong one as a child, the healthy one. She'd been the one adopted. Raised by a wealthy family. Engaged to marry a man who loved her.

Yet things weren't always as they seemed. If Sylvie had learned anything in the last few days, that was it. "We aren't going to be victims, Diana. We'll find a way out."

"Professor Bertram has lost his mind. I've tried everything I can think of to—"

A metallic rattle cut the darkness. A door creaked open. A shadow loomed against the twilight sky, broad shoulders filling the doorway.

Bryce

You have no idea of the horror I've been through. My life is over. Ruined. And he will never pay. Not enough. So you will pay for him.

The contents of the letter scrolled over and over in Bryce's mind. How could he have been so stupid as to assume the letter was written by Ed Dryden? Had he been that obsessed with the serial killer? Had he been that blind?

Of course, he never guessed Sylvie and Diana were Dryden's daughters. He still had trouble wrapping his mind around that. It didn't seem possible that monster was related to Sylvie in any way.

Bryce set the letter on the desk and started paging through the photocopied articles in Diana Gale's folder, frustration pounding in his ears. When he'd told Val and Perreth his reasons for believing Professor Bertram had been the kidnapper and not a victim, it hadn't occurred to him that he wouldn't be going with them, that he wouldn't be able to personally make sure Sylvie was safe.

He knew that shouldn't matter, that he should be content that they'd listened to him, that they were checking Bertram's apartment right now along with his office, his wife's house, and a vacation home along Lake Wisconsin. That they were using all the resources at law enforcements' fingertips.

But contentment was far beyond him.

At least they'd allowed him to stay in Sylvie's hotel room. At least here he could fool himself into thinking he was doing something to help. That in case they failed to find Sylvie at any of the professor's properties, Bryce could come up with an answer. A place to look that no one had thought of.

He skimmed article after article. Dryden had killed so many women. The blond coeds he'd practiced on before working up his courage to kill his wife. The brunette he'd killed to send a message to Professor Risa Madsen and his failed attempt on Risa herself. Three different locations. All remote. All wooded.

The professor's cabin was the best bet. He'd probably take them there. But if he hadn't...

Bryce paged backward, to the deaths of the coeds. A picture of Dawn Bertram smiled up at him, her face in negative, an effect of the microfilm machine.

Tearing his gaze from the girl's face, he focused on the article. Dawn's body had been discovered in a gravel quarry west of Eau Claire. The police reported that she hadn't been killed there, that she had been moved.

He paged on. Through the story of one girl after another. Each leaving family and loved ones looking for answers.

An empty ache hollowed out under his rib cage. Dryden's depravities had been like a stone thrown into a still pond, the ever-widening ripple caused by each murder ruining so many lives. Those who suffered the death of a daughter, a sister, a mother. Those who weren't old enough to understand all they'd lost.

Bertram was one of his victims. Sylvie too. And later, even Bryce. Everyone who came into contact with Dryden was damaged in some way. Bertram chose to pass the pain on.

Bryce focused on the grainy photo of Trent Burnell, the FBI profiler whose work had led to Dryden's capture. He stood near a cabin. A cabin rimmed with tall pine trees.

A cabin that might still be there.

Adrenaline slammed into Bryce's system. He skimmed the article. Dryden had killed Sylvie's mother at that cabin, and that was where he'd been caught. Although it had never been proven, it was possible Dawn Bertram and the other coeds were hunted there as well.

It was possible.

He had to call Perreth.

Bryce grabbed his phone, but instead of punching in the detective's number, he searched for the location given in the article. The sun was setting now. It would be night when he reached Dryden's old hunting grounds. He would call from the road.

There was no time to lose.

Especially since he had a stop to make on the way. A visit with a client he'd once defended—a gun collector who lived just outside of Lake Loyal.

Sylvie

Sylvie blinked as bright light flooded the cabin from the naked bulb overhead. Professor Bertram was back.

He'd been in and out of the cabin over the last few hours. Checking to see if she was awake. Testing the ropes. Cleaning and loading a rifle. This time he was dressed in a black turtleneck and black jeans. He entered the room holding a pair of strange-looking goggles. A sheathed knife hung at his belt. A rifle was slung across his back.

He'd refused to answer her questions in his prior visits. But that didn't mean she was going to quit asking. "What are you going to do?"

He turned to her, surprised, as if he'd forgotten she was there. Or maybe he'd just forgotten she and Diana were human. "It's time for the hunt."

"The hunt?"

Bertram nodded. He turned to look at her with sunken eyes. He obviously hadn't shaved since she'd first seen him, his chin covered in silver bristle that sparkled in the naked light. "He hunted my daughter. My Dawn. He tied her in a cabin. Tortured her. Humiliated her. Then hunted her like an animal."

Sylvie couldn't believe what she was hearing. "You're going to hunt *us*?"

He pulled a knife out of its sheath and held it in shaking hands. The light caught the edge of the blade. "Not me. Not me. Him. It's what he did."

"That was a long time ago. It doesn't have to happen again. You're—"

Bertram turned bloodshot eyes on her. "It has to happen. Just the same. It's the only way to make him pay. The only way."

A feeling colder than the uninsulated cabin sank into Sylvie's gut. Diana was right. Somewhere between grief and bitterness and obsession, Bertram had lost it.

He circled to Diana's bed. Lowering the knife to her chest, he slipped the blade between Diana's collarbone and the lace of her dress and pulled it upward, slitting the bodice.

Sylvie fought to control her panic. She couldn't let him take Diana first. She'd been tied in the cabin for three days with little food or water. She was too weak to run, too weak to escape. At times when they'd been talking, she'd seemed confused, disoriented. She'd be no match for Bertram. If he took her out of this cabin, Sylvie would never see her again.

"Take me first."

Diana thrashed her head back and forth. "Don't listen to her. I started this. Sylvie didn't even know Ed Dryden was our father. You know that. I was the one who tracked him down. She's only here because of me."

"No, Diana." Sylvie injected as much urgency into her voice as she could. Diana thought she was helping, but she was signing her own death warrant. "I just saw Dryden today."

"I'm the one he knows best. Sylvie was the sick one. He had no use for her. I was always his favorite."

"Damn it, Diana. Don't do this."

"It's only right."

Bertram ignored them both. He sliced through the rest of Diana's dress and undergarments. He spread open the fabric, unveiling bare skin to the harsh overhead glare.

His throat worked as if he was trying to swallow but couldn't. Sweat beaded on his forehead and trickled down one gray temple. He averted his eyes, as if looking at Diana's naked body would be impolite.

Sylvie watched him, recognizing the battle going on in his mind. The man wasn't a murderer. The guilt stemming from what he was about to do seemed to be wearing him down. And if that was the case, maybe Sylvie and Diana could appeal to him yet. Maybe they could both walk away. "You don't have to do this. There has to be another way."

He cocked his head to one side. "Another way?"

"Yes." She scrambled for something to say, anything. "You... You can talk to Dryden. Make him see what he's done."

"Don't you think I've tried that? He laughed at me. He laughed. And then after that first time, he refused to face me. I tried for almost twenty years."

"What if I asked him to see you? Diana and I can both ask."

"He'll listen to us," Diana added. "I know he will."

Bertram paused, then he shook his head. "It's no use."

"Why give up before we even try?"

"You forget. I know Dryden. If he realized you were asking on my behalf, he'd only figure out a way to string me out, give me hope so he could dash it. He'd just want to see me suffer more." The professor shook his head slowly and mumbled. "No more. No more."

Sylvie chewed the inside of her lip. He was probably right, but she couldn't admit it. She wasn't about to consign both Diana and herself to death.

All Bertram could think about was himself. All he could feel was his own pain. On some level, he'd become everything he hated. And if he murdered Diana and her in cold blood, he'd cross the line for good. He'd become Ed Dryden.

And maybe that was the way to reach him.

"I feel for you, Professor," Sylvie said, trying to be convincing. "I really do. But you can't kill us. You're not like Dryden. You're not a murderer."

"But I am."

His confession hit her between the eyes. How could she have forgotten? The shouting on the road. The rapid pops. "The officers."

Bertram shook his head. "They're not dead. At least not yet. I heard a report on the radio on the drive up."

Thank God. "Bryce's brother? Did you kill Tanner Walker?"

He looked at her as if he thought the suggestion preposterous. "Of course not."

"Then... how are you a murderer? I don't understand."

He looked down at the floor. "You should. You found his body."

Sylvie didn't have to try very hard to remember the smell of death, the sight of his eyes. "Sami."

Diana gasped. "You killed Sami Yamal?"

"He was going to the police. I couldn't let..." He touched his fingers to his forehead as if trying to quell a headache.

"So he didn't commit suicide."

"I needed time."

Time so he could kidnap her. Time so he could kill her and Diana.

"I didn't want to do it. I didn't want to do any of this." A dry sob broke from his lips. He slid his hand over his mouth.

Sylvie was getting close to convincing him. She could feel it. All she needed to do was to keep talking. "See? You're not a murderer. Sami's death is eating you up."

"Ed Dryden stole my Dawn. My brilliant little girl. He doesn't deserve daughters. Beautiful daughters." He finally let his gaze skitter over Diana's naked body. "Not when he took mine."

It all went back to Ed Dryden. To events they had nothing to do with. A man they had no control over. "We were three years old when he was arrested. We don't even remember him."

Setting his lips in a determined line, Bertram slit the ropes tying Diana's arms and legs to the bedframe. Pulling off the sliced dress, he retied her wrists in front of her and pulled her up out of the bed.

Diana swayed on her feet. "Please."

"You can't do this," Sylvie said.

"Shut up. You have to shut up. If I could make him pay without hurting you, I would. If I could make him sorry for what he did. But he's not sorry. He's never going to be sorry."

Sylvie couldn't argue with that either. That man... her father might not even be capable of remorse.

But Bertram was.

"I know you have your reasons. But by killing us, you prove that you're just as bad as Ed Dryden. Just as evil. How are you planning to live with yourself?"

He stared at her with dead eyes. "I'm not."

Diana

Professor Bertram opened the cabin door and grabbed Diana by one arm.

Diana took one look back at her sister. She wanted to say so much. Tell Sylvie how special she was. How finding her had brightened Diana's life. How much she wished they had more time together. But the only words she could manage to form were I'm sorry, and even then, her voice wouldn't come.

Bertram pushed her outside, slammed the door behind them, and marched her across the clearing to the woods.

The moon glowed with a cold light, and Diana's breath fogged in the air. She had been tied in the bed so long that her legs tingled with the sudden increase in blood flow. Pinecones and sticks dug into the soles of her feet. She stumbled, regained her footing, then stumbled again.

Bertram held her upright, his fingers digging into her arm. When they reached the tree line, he stopped and released her. "Run."

Diana's legs wobbled under her. She took two steps, then fell to her knees, catching herself with her elbows, wrists still tied tight.

"It's time to begin. Get up."

She managed to rise to her knees.

Bertram loomed over her. "I won't shoot you. Not if I don't have to."

Diana eyed the rifle, still slung across his back. She wasn't sure what he wanted her to say, so she said nothing.

"He didn't shoot my Dawn. He caught her with his bare hands. And then he used a knife." He touched the sheath on his belt.

"Please," Diana doubted he'd listen, but she had to try. "You can do whatever you want to me... anything... just leave Sylvie out of this. Please."

Bertram looked her over for a moment, as if imagining what her offer might entail. Then he turned away. "I can do whatever I want to you both. And I want you to run."

"Leave Sylvie—"

"I said run."

Diana scrambled to her unsteady feet and ran.

Sylvie

Dizziness swept over Sylvie. She gripped the mattress with tied hands, trying to hold on, to steady herself, to keep from falling into panic. But holding on couldn't steady her. Nothing could steady her. Not with Diana out there in the night. Not with the professor hunting her.

Sylvie had to get free. But how?

Calm.

Think.

Sylvie looked around the cabin. Bertram had left the light on, giving her the first good look at the place. Unfortunately, she couldn't see much that would help. The room was bare. Only the two mattresses, musty pillows, and shades covering the windows.

In the next room she could see what looked like a kitchen area with wood-burning stove in the far corner. There might be a knife or scissors in the kitchen or something sharp or heavy in the vicinity of the stove. Of course, she couldn't reach it, not tied as she was to the bed.

Raising her head from the pillow, she looked down at her hands. White cord of the type used for clotheslines wrapped her arms just above her wrists, tying each to the bed frame. She could hardly move her hands. There was no way she could work them free. She'd be willing to bet Diana had spent days trying.

Just the thought of Diana scrambling for her life, weak and naked in the darkness, made the dizziness start all over again.

Calm.

Think.

Sylvie studied the rope again, straining her neck, her abdominal muscles shaking with the effort of raising her body from the pillow. When Bertram had tied her, he hadn't pulled the cord tight against her skin. Instead he'd tied it over the sleeves of her chunky knit sweater.

She let her head fall back to the pillow. If she could stretch the sweater and work a sleeve out from under the rope, she might have enough wiggle room to get free.

It was sure worth a try.

Sylvie turned her head to the side. Bending her neck, she grasped her sweater between her teeth and pulled.

The cotton stretched. Little by little, she could feel it slip against her skin and out from under the tight cord.

She gathered more of the knitted cotton into her mouth. More slipped under the rope.

Almost there.

Leaning her head back, she bit down and tugged as hard

as she could. Her teeth ached. The skin on her arm burned. Finally, the sleeve pulled free.

She spit the dry cotton from her mouth. So far so good. Gritting her teeth, she pulled her arm up, working the bit of slack over her wrist.

Over her hand.

Free.

Blood rushed through her hand. Shaking out the burn and tingle, she made short work of the rope securing the other hand. Then she turned to freeing her feet.

Sylvie climbed from the bed and moved to the kitchen area as fast as she could on tingling feet. She yanked open a drawer.

Empty.

She opened another and another until she'd checked every drawer and cabinet in the small area. Each one was empty. She would have to find something outside. She would have to improvise.

Outside the night was dark, and her eyes struggled to adjust. The slight glow of the slivered moon through leafless branches. The hulking black pine and fir. Steam rose into the night with each breath.

Sylvie had to be careful. She'd be willing to bet the strange-looking goggles she had seen Bertram carry into the cabin were for night vision. He'd be able to see her long before she could spot him.

Leaves and twigs crackled under her shoes, making her flinch with each step. She had no idea how many acres of forest stretched around them. She wasn't even sure where they were. All she could see was forest. All she could smell were fallen leaves and evergreen. But it hadn't taken too long to untie herself. With any luck, Diana and Bertram would still be nearby.

She needed a weapon.

Searching the forest floor, Sylvie spotted a good-sized branch. She picked it up, shook it a little to test it. Heavy, but not too heavy. It was no rifle, but it would have to do. She had no better choice.

She crept around a clump of bushes. Twigs scratched at her sweater and clawed through her hair. Even though it was nearing winter, the forest felt alive. Eyes were watching. Human or animal, she couldn't tell.

Sylvie could see a clearing open beyond the brush, knee-high grass glowing blue in the moonlight. Out in the open, she would be an easy target. Her only hope was to stay in the forest. At least she had shoes and jeans and a thick sweater to protect her from the brush and thorns.

For Diana, the forest would be difficult going. She had to find her sister before it was—

A scream shredded the air.

Too late.

Bryce

Bryce swept his flashlight over footings that had once served as a cabin's foundation. Grass grew high around the lichen-covered concrete. A white wooden cross and a bouquet of battered fake flowers leaned against one of the footings, the faded shrine of long-ago murders.

He'd called Perreth on the way up, once it was too late for the detective to stop him. Now he regretted it. Instead of helping, he'd diverted the detective's attention, making him waste resources investigating a weather-beaten memorial and the foundation of a cabin that was no more.

Bryce walked back to his car. Maybe they'd already found

Sylvie. Maybe it was already over. Taking one last look around the pine and hickory and glowing white skeletons of birch, he lowered himself into the car and pulled out his phone.

A scream ripped through the forest.

Sylvie. She was here.

He grabbed his new rifle from the back seat, thrust himself out of the car, and raced toward the sound. He moved quickly through the barren understory of pine and fir. But before long the landscape changed. More deciduous trees took over the forest. Their leafless branches stretched to the starry sky, affording more light. But brush began to crowd his path. Thorny branches of wild blackberry ripped at his jeans.

By the time Bryce spotted the log cabin, he was thoroughly out of breath. A light glowed bright around window shades and through small chinks in the cabin's wall. A van parked in front of it, the same van he'd tried to rescue Sylvie from yesterday morning.

So he was right after all. Well, sort of. Only it wasn't the cabin itself that was important. It was the forest. The same forest where Dryden had hunted Bertram's daughter.

Val's search for property owned by Bertram hadn't listed this place. But there had to be some way he knew it would be vacant. Either he rented it, or... A sign out front explained it all.

Sami's Sanctuary.

Bryce doubted it was an accident that Sami Yamal bought a cabin near Dryden's hunting grounds. And that Bertram took advantage of it. If Yamal hadn't been so bitter toward Bertram, Bryce might have wondered if they were in on this together.

Obsession layered upon obsession.

Bryce crept toward the cabin, his rifle at the ready. It had been years since he'd last gone deer hunting with Tanner, and the weapon felt awkward in his hands. It had never been his thing from the beginning. The great outdoors. Shooting things. He'd preferred boating and fishing. He was pretty sure he could shoot Bertram though. Just line up the bastard and take him down.

The professor never should have threatened Sylvie.

Reaching the door, Bryce leaned close to its rough surface and listened. No voices. No movement. He reached for the rusty knob. Tested it. It moved under his fingers.

One...

Two...

Three...

Bryce twisted the doorknob and shoved. He lunged into the cabin, rifle at his shoulder, and swept the small space with his gun. A kitchen filled one side of the room, furnished with table, chairs, and an old wood stove. A battered couch lined the opposite wall.

Vacant.

He focused on an open door. Bathroom? Bedroom?

Stepping as quietly as he could, he inched to the side until he could see inside. Two twin beds lined the walls, mattresses bare except for a shabby pillow on each. Ropes tangled from bed frames. And on the floor lay the shredded remnants of a bridal gown.

The scream he'd heard must have come from outside.

The hunt had already begun.

Val

"You missed the turn." Val said, watching the green road

sign slip into the darkness behind Stan Perreth's car.

The detective gave her a dismissive glance. "Did not."

"Yeah, you did."

"I'm going a different way."

"Why, you felt like taking a long cut?"

Perreth grunted. "This is probably a wild goose chase, you know. That cabin was torn down years ago."

"Then why did you insist on coming with me?"

At least two miles hummed under the tires before he answered. "I thought it would give us, you know…"

Val tensed. "No. I don't know."

"Some time together."

"Are you nuts, Stan? I explained this to you. I'm engaged."

"You didn't say happily engaged. That's a tell."

Val rolled her eyes so hard it gave her a headache. "Are you really going to make me come out and say it?

"Say what?"

"It's not going to happen, Stan."

"Then why lead me on?"

"Lead you on?" Val shook her head. She could see now that there was no winning for her here. Stan would insist she was into him until she offended him, and then he'd be angry. She'd tried to navigate this mine field plenty of times before. It always led to an explosion. "Let's focus on the case."

"I told you, the cabin isn't there anymore."

"Bryce thinks there's something to it. I'm inclined to believe him."

"Over believing me?"

"I got it. The cabin isn't there. I believe you. But if Bertram is our man, and he's trying to pay Dryden back, it makes sense that he'd come here. He wasn't at his properties. He hasn't used his credit card. And I didn't ask you to come up. I just didn't want Bryce to have to handle it alone, just in case he's right. He's no cop."

"Neither are you."

He didn't have to remind her, but Val didn't see the upside to pointing that out.

But Stan wasn't finished. "Where did he keep Diana Gale all this time? The trunk of his car? It's not logical to drive all the way up here when he doesn't even have a place to stay."

"Revenge has its own emotional logic."

"Oh, I see. It's a woman's intuition thing. Hell hath no fury, and all that."

Val fought to keep from rolling her eyes. "No, it's more like crazy powerful witch magic. Turn here."

He followed her direction this time. A mile later, they reached the road Bryce had told them about and took a right, plunging into forest.

They drove another several miles, the road edging lakes and wetlands, and delving deeper into a mix of evergreen and deciduous trees that gave the Northwoods its name. To Val's relief, Perreth didn't talk, probably content to just stew and think up new slights to salve his ego. Val was about to switch on the radio when a high screech pierced the quiet.

"Was that an owl?" Perreth asked.

Val brushed her hand along the holster at her waist that held her personal weapon, reassuring herself it was there. "That sounded like a scream."

SYLVIE

Sylvie raced in the direction of the scream.

She spotted them on the clearing's edge. Diana knelt in the tall grass. Bertram stood over her, his fist tangled in her hair. A knife blade gleamed in his hand. The rifle was slung across his shoulder.

Adrenaline slammed through Sylvie so hard she felt dizzy. She wanted to scream, launch herself at him, rip out his eyes with her fingernails. But she had to be smart about this. One slash of the blade, and Diana would be dead. And if he decided to use the rifle...

Sylvie gripped the branch, her palms sweaty, and circled toward them through the edge of the woods. She moved as fast as she dared. Creeping up behind him, she raised the branch to her shoulder.

He was five steps away.

Four.

Three.

He turned his head, as if he'd heard a sound.

Two steps.

He spotted her. His eyes grew wide.

One.

Letting out a bellow, she swung the branch like a baseball bat, aiming at his head. It connected. The blow shuddered up her arms.

Bertram released Diana. He spun to fully face Sylvie, the knife blade ready in his hand.

"No!" Diana screamed. She grabbed Bertram's legs from behind.

"Diana, run!" Sylvie swung again.

Bertram dodged to the side.

The branch missed, its momentum throwing Sylvie off balance. "Run!" she screamed at her sister. "Run!"

Diana stumbled to her feet.

The professor reached for her.

Sylvie swung again.

But this time, Bertram was ready. He grabbed the branch and twisted it. He was strong, too strong. He wrenched the weapon from Sylvie's grasp and threw it to the ground.

Diana was stumbling forward, moving, but slow. Sylvie had to keep Bertram busy long enough for Diana to get away.

She lashed out with a foot, kicking Bertram's thigh.

He grabbed her ankle and pulled.

Sylvie fell backward and hit the ground. The force jutted up her spine and slammed her teeth together.

"Goddammit." Bertram loomed over her, his face contorted with rage. He pulled back a foot and plowed it into her ribs.

Sylvie gasped for air, the force of the fall still clanging through her head. Now she was the one in danger. She had to clear her head. Get to her feet. *Run.*

Pushing herself into a crouch, she looked up...

...and into the barrel of Bertram's rifle. Eyes hidden by night-vision goggles and face twisted with anger, the professor looked inhuman. Monstrous. Insane. "Go ahead and scream. No one can hear you. That's why he brought them here, you know. So he could enjoy their screams. Revel in their fear."

"You enjoy it too, don't you?" Sylvie knew she should shut her mouth, that she risked making him angrier. But she couldn't help it. She'd had enough of this bullshit. *Enough.* "You really are just like him."

Bertram flinched. "I'm nothing like him. I don't want to do this. I have no choice."

Fear no longer rang in her ears, no longer pinched the back of her neck. She'd had it with Bertram. His self-pity. His excuses. She wanted to shove his words down his throat and make him choke on them. "It's time you stop blaming Dryden for everything you do. It's time you stop letting him determine your life. It's time you stand on your own goddamn feet."

"Shut up and take off your clothes."

"Pervert."

"Not me. Dryden. He cut off their clothes with a knife. He made them... he humiliated them. My Dawn. He... he did shameful things."

"He has nothing to do with this. You want to—"

"Take them off. I don't want to shoot you yet, but I will. I can still hunt your sister. She's easy enough to catch."

"Oh, so doing exactly what Dryden did isn't that important. Just the me getting naked part."

His lips twisted in something resembling a snarl.

"This isn't about revenge. You just want to do every little shameful thing you've been obsessing about all these years. But you're not honest enough to own it. Yeah, that's right. I didn't think you had the—"

Reaching out, the professor clamped down on Sylvie's throat.

She gasped, struggling for air.

Oh, shit. Maybe she'd underestimated him. Maybe...

He brought the knife to her throat.

So this was how it would end? Right here in the clearing? Naked and defiled at the hands of this delusional asshole?

Bertram slipped the blade under the scoop neck of her sweater and slit the fabric open. He fumbled with the knife, trying to slip it between the cups of her bra.

Summoning all her strength, Sylvie plowed her foot backward. And the same time, she pushed his arm away as best she could.

He grunted. The knife fell into the tall grass.

She kicked again. Harder.

He staggered back. Released her throat.

She twisted and ran, dashing across the opening. Racing for the cover of brush and trees. Zigzagging as much as she could to keep him from getting a clear shot.

Gunfire split the air.

Sylvie tensed, waiting for the bullet's sting. Waiting for the force of it to knock her to the ground.

Waiting for all of it to be over.

Bryce

Bryce had barely realized his shot missed when Bertram spun around, crouched down in the grass, and started firing back.

A bullet whizzed past Bryce's ear.

He hit the ground, his pulse thundering in his ears, his whole body shaking. He wasn't a good shot. Not like his little brother. But when he'd seen the professor raise his rifle to his shoulder and train the barrel on Sylvie as she was running away, he'd just fired.

Now with no cover except tall grass—which was no real cover at all—he was up shit creek.

But wait...

So was Bertram.

Bryce slowed his breathing.

In and out.

In and out.

He might only get one shot. He had to make it count.

He snugged the rifle to his shoulder. He put his finger on the trigger. He counted off the seconds in his head.

One.

Two.

On three, he rose from the grass, spotted Bertram coming toward him, and fired.

Blam.

Blam.

Blam.

The professor fell backwards.

Bryce ducked back down in the grass. Did he hit him? Was Bertram hurt? Dead? He peeked over the wispy seed heads, but he couldn't see anything but more grass.

He wasn't sure how long he waited, but it seemed like hours. Finally he stood and walked cautiously across the clearing.

Bryce spotted an indentation in the vegetation. He kept the rifle at his shoulder. If Bertram was playing him, he needed to be ready to fire back.

He stepped closer.

Closer.

The first thing he noticed was darkness. It stained the grass' silvery leaves. Then he made out Bertram himself.

The professor lay on his back, his chest dark and shiny. Blood. And lots of it. His breathing was fast, a loud sort of wheezing.

Did I do this?

Bryce heard a sound behind him. He started, spun around—

"It's Val. It's Val Ryker. It's okay." The former cop held her hands up. As soon as she saw that he recognized her, she lowered them to her sides.

"Oh, shit." Val darted around him and dropped to her knees beside the professor. She moved the rifle away from him, then shucked her jacket, wadded it up, and pressed it to

Bertram's chest. She put her fingers to this throat, checking for a pulse. "Hang in there, Professor."

Bertram didn't answer, his chest making that wheezing, sucking sound.

Bryce couldn't move. He just stared. When he'd pulled the trigger, he'd known what he was doing. He'd wanted to destroy this man. But now? Watching him struggle, witnessing his pain, Bryce felt sick.

"We called the locals. They should be on their way. But it wouldn't hurt to call again."

Bryce heard Val talking, but it took him a few seconds to grasp her words. "What?"

"Call 911."

Bertram's breathing slowed, the sucking sound growing weaker. Bit by bit, the life seemed to leach from his staring eyes.

Bryce pulled out his phone. "No signal."

"Shit."

Perreth caught up with them. He looked down at Val. "Dead?"

"Near."

"You got him?" the detective asked Val. "I'm going to track down Diana Gale. She's got to be around here somewhere."

Val nodded. "I got him."

Perreth marched off into the woods.

Val looked up at Bryce. Blood soaked through the wadded-up jacket, turning her hands red. The sucking sound had all but stopped.

"Did you see where Sylvie went?" Val asked.

Bryce nodded.

"Go after her."

"I've never shot any—" The words caught in his throat. All

the times he'd fantasized about killing Dryden these last months. How eager he'd been to shoot Bertram. And now?

Now he just felt empty.

"He was going to kill Sylvie," Val said. "That's defense of others."

"I know." He'd studied the law. He'd practiced. But this... watching a death he'd caused was different. Horrible. "I'm not worried about the legal implications."

"It changes you, killing someone. Damages you. And it takes time to come to terms with it. But it will work out. Now go find Sylvie."

Sylvie.

Yes, he had to find Sylvie. And once he did, he'd never let her go.

That was the only way any of this would work out.

Diana

Stars and moon glowed in the sky. Shadow puddled under pine.

Diana huddled in a small hollow. She knew the surrounding thicket wasn't enough to hide her. Not with the moonlight so bright. But she couldn't run. Couldn't even walk. Not one more step.

Her skin stung with scratches and cuts. Her legs ached to the bone. Her whole body trembled. The rope still bound her wrists, so tight it chafed her skin. She'd tried rubbing it on a rock, but it barely frayed. She'd tried to use a stick to pry at it, but all she'd done was gouge her arm.

She'd been crying since she heard the gunshots, and she couldn't stop. It seemed as though she'd been crying for days.

Bertram had night-vision goggles. Bertram had a gun.

And when Diana had last seen Sylvie, she'd held only a branch.

It wasn't hard to guess how those shots had turned out.

Diana had pulled Sylvie into this mess, and all her sister had focused on was saving her. And now... now Diana supposed none of it mattered. Either Bertram would find her and gut her with his knife, or she would die of thirst or cold. And there wasn't anything she could do.

Nearby, a twig snapped. Leaves crunched under boots. The silhouette of a man fought through brush, growing closer. Closer.

He stopped.

It was almost over.

Diana grabbed a stick in both hands. She got ready to strike. The least she could do was hurt him. Hurt him like he'd hurt her sister.

"Diana? Diana Gale?"

She didn't recognize his voice, but it sure wasn't Vincent Bertram.

"It's okay. It's okay. It's over. You can come out."

Diana held the stick in front of her like a sword. "Who are you?"

"Police. Detective Stan Perreth, Madison PD."

The name sounded familiar, but Diana couldn't place it. All she could focus on was the word police. "My sister..."

"I know. I know. Sylvie. We found her."

"Is she—"

"She's fine. She's safe."

Oh, thank God.

"And the professor?"

"He was shot."

"Dead?"

"By now? Probably."

Diana let out a shuddering breath. She supposed she should feel something. Elation? Sadness? Relief?

All she felt was numb.

"You want to come out of there?" he said.

Diana nodded, but she couldn't manage to move.

He held out a hand. "Come on. It's okay. Come with me, and I'll get you someplace safe. I'll take you to your sister."

Diana reached out.

The detective took her hand and led her out of the thicket. He circled an arm around her, assisting her, his hand low on her waist.

Finally she stood upright on trembling legs. Her skin glowed, naked in the moonlight, streaked with red scratches and blood.

"Here. Let me help." The detective shrugged off his jacket and draped it over her shoulders, holding the fabric open. "Is this okay?"

She nodded.

"You sure?"

"Yes. Thank you."

But instead of closing the coat, he paused, taking another long look. When he finally wrapped it around her and zipped it up, he took his time, skimming her breasts with his fingertips, slowing when he reached her nipples.

Diana couldn't think, couldn't feel. She just stood there and didn't say a word. If she'd ever really had any fight in her, it was gone now. Lost in that cabin in the dark or ripped out of her by brambles in the forest.

After all that had happened in the past days, this cop's awkward fumbling was nothing. He wasn't going to hunt her. Wasn't going to kill her or her sister. Wasn't going to gut her in some twisted attempt to get back at a father she wished she never knew. He could look and touch all he wanted, if that's what it took for her to get home.

And once she did, she'd make sure she was never this weak again.

SYLVIE

"Sylvie! Sylvie!" His voice was far away, still in the clearing, but Sylvie would recognize it from any distance.

Bryce.

She peered out from behind the thick trunk of a cedar. Starlight glowed in the clearing, turning the grass silvery. The silhouette of a man strode toward her. Broad shoulders. Too tall for Bertram.

It could only be Bryce.

"The professor, he has a rifle."

"He's dead, Sylvie. Bertram is dead."

She closed her eyes and clung to the rough bark, her whole body shaking. She'd been fighting so hard, the thought that she didn't have to fight any more left her weak. Pulling in a deep breath, she pushed away from the tree and picked through the edge of the forest, making her way toward Bryce.

"Diana?"

"Detective Perreth and Val Ryker are here. Perreth is looking for her. Don't worry, Sylvie, he'll find her. Bertram didn't get her."

She looked past Bryce's shoulder and into the clearing, toward where she'd last seen her sister. It seemed so long since she knew Diana was okay. Tears blurred her vision, turning the night into a mosaic of light and dark. "Are you sure?"

"I'm sure."

Reaching her, he engulfed her in his arms.

Sylvie pressed her cheek to his shoulder and held on. She didn't know why he was here, why he'd come back to her. It was enough to know that he had.

She wasn't sure how long they stood there, clinging to each other, but finally Bryce stepped back, still grasping her hands, and looked into her eyes. "There's so much I need to say."

Sylvie held her breath. She had no idea what to expect, good or bad, loving or regretful. But whatever it was, it wouldn't change anything she felt. She'd lived too long in her protective cocoon, afraid to risk, afraid to have her heart broken. And what had it gained her? A lonely life where she had acquaintances instead of friends. A sister who was afraid to tell her the truth. A secret of her own that had almost died with her.

She'd had it with safe. She'd had it with secrets. She'd had it with holding back. "I love you, Bryce."

He stared at her, as if her pronouncement had shocked all thought from his mind. "I... love you, too."

"You do?"

"Yes. Yes."

She threw herself back into his arms and kissed him. Hungry and overjoyed and so relieved she could barely stand.

The kissed for a long time, not able to get enough of each other, not able to stop. And when they finally came up for air, Bryce looked down at her, his expression so serious that for a moment, Sylvie was afraid again.

"What is it? What's wrong?"

"I'm so sorry I was such an ass."

Sylvie let out a shaky breath. "You were kind of an ass."

She hadn't meant it as a joke, but when it came out, it was so direct and even a little cruel, that she couldn't help but follow it with a short laugh.

"It's not funny."

"It's kind of funny."

"I left you in the lurch."

"I told you that you would. I'm always right. You should listen to me."

"There's no excuse. I was shocked and angry and I totally screwed up, but none of that should have been aimed at you. That was stupid. It was all so stupid."

"Yeah, it was pretty stupid." Sylvie could barely contain the laughter now. Tears streamed down her cheeks.

"You seem to be enjoying this."

"I am."

"I just want you to know I mean it, Sylvie. I'm so sorry I let Dryden or anything else come between us, even for a moment."

"You came back. You saved my life. You're here now." Just when she'd needed him most. He hadn't let her down after all.

"And I'm never going to leave." He kissed her again, wrapping her in warmth, holding her close. "I never stopped loving you, Sylvie. Not for a second. I want you to know that."

"I know." And she did.

"Do you really?"

"Yeah."

"I realize we've only known each other a few days, but..." He pulled back from her and looked into her eyes, a smile on his face this time, one so bright it stole her breath. "I propose a new deal."

"Will I like the terms?"

"If you don't, you can change them at any time."

"Okay, what's your offer, counselor?"

"I propose we take our time, get to know one another."

"Sounds like a plan."

"We don't want to rush into anything."

"No, we wouldn't want that."

"And then, after a good amount of time has passed, if we are still as happy—or happier—than we are right now, we talk about making things permanent."

Sylvie couldn't hold back the laughter. "Like white-dress-and-matching-wedding-bands permanent?"

"The whole package. White dress, matching wedding bands, and children of our own. I can see it right now. Can you? A family."

Sylvie closed her eyes. Marriage. A family. The sheerest cliff there was. The most dangerous fall. The sharpest rocks waiting below.

Opening her eyes, she looked into the face of the man she loved, the man she'd never dared to dream of finding. The risk might be daunting, but the payoff was extraordinary.

And she was up to the challenge.

Val

Eight days later.

Val rewound footage from the meeting between Sylvie and Ed Dryden for what had to be the fiftieth time.

Sitting beside her in the sheriff's department office, Bobby Vaughan nodded his head. "Again, if you wouldn't mind."

"Are you committing it to memory?"

"If it will help find the damn copycat."

He had a point. Although some of the forensics had

started to trickle in, they were woefully behind on knowledge when it came to Dryden. There was a lot of catching up to do. Still... "Some sleep might help. You look awful."

"Thanks."

"Seriously, Bobby. You got out of the hospital less than a week ago. When was the last time you spent more than six hours at home?"

"I can do more good here."

Val studied him for a moment. Bobby tended to be obsessive about his work, but this was different. And Val was pretty sure she knew the cause. "So Diana hasn't changed her mind."

Bobby shook his head. "It's over."

"I'm sorry. Want to talk about it?"

"No."

"Sure?"

He focused on the computer screen, his face an emotionless mask. "Play it again. There must be something we're missing."

Val clicked play, and the hypnotic voice of Ed Dryden filled the office one more time.

"I'm sorry I have to let you down, Sylvie. But I don't know where your sister is."

"Please. You're a powerful man. I know you're in touch with someone outside of prison."

"Why would you think that?"

"I... I just do."

"And you think I asked someone to take Diana?"

"Did you?"

"I expected more from you."

"Please answer my question."

"I didn't have anything to do with your sister's disappearance. I have no reason to want to hurt her."

"Two women have been murdered recently. They were killed in the same way you killed your victims. The same exact way."

"And what way is that?"

"I don't think you need me to tell you what you already know."

"No. But I do need you to tell me why you think Diana is among these women. That's why you're here, right? You think Diana is the third? Or you're afraid she will be?"

Diana

Eight months later.

Diana Gale clutched the loosely wrapped bouquet of spring daisies in her hands and took her measured walk down the garden path. The June sun warmed her back. The scent of iris and peony hung sweet in the air, their blooms framing simple rows of chairs filled with smiling people. A guitar's simple strum blended with snatches of birdsong.

Diana reached her spot next to the minister and gave Bryce a generous smile. Dashing yet relaxed in his gray stroller, he looked happy. There was no hint of his ongoing hunt for his brother's murderer, the man the media now called The Copycat Killer. No sign of the stresses that had played out in that forest many months ago. His hazel eyes were so focused on his future with Sylvie, his handsome face so at ease and sparkling with hope, it made Diana's chest ache.

On the other hand, since the night Sylvie and she had walked away from that cabin in the north woods, Diana had struggled to put her life back together. Never again would she let herself depend on others for safety and strength. Never again would she let herself be so weak, so vulnerable. She'd been a victim since she was a child, but now—no matter how difficult life became—it was time to stand on her own feet, make her own decisions.

Facing her own weakness and dependence had been hard. Facing Bobby had been harder. It seemed as if he'd always been there for her. Protecting her. Taking care of her. And she'd always let him. He hadn't understood why she couldn't let him anymore.

Diana swallowed into an aching throat. She couldn't think about Bobby. She couldn't think about her own struggles. At least not today. Today she would push the worries aside. She'd made it through the winter, and now it was time to appreciate the new life of spring.

And what better way to do that than by enjoying her sister's wedding?

Diana turned to look up the garden aisle just as Sylvie walked toward them. Her flowing white gown of silk chiffon wisped around her ankles. The sunlight played across the white lace bow in her hair. And on her lips danced the most glorious smile as she strode forward to claim her future.

I HOPE you are enjoying Small Town Secrets: Sins. For a sneak peek at the next book in the series, turn the page!

FRANTIC
(Small Town Secrets: Sins, Book 3)

THE COPYCAT KILLER

Laundromats made good hunting grounds.

Alone, for now, he sat back to wait, listening to the empty rumble of the dryer and the tinny radio tuned to the blues. He liked a little blues on a hunting trip. The music was gritty and real and full of pain. Like the sweetness of a dying scream.

He'd never guessed how invincible killing could make him feel. The godlike power of holding life and death in his hands. It had taken a mentor to teach him. To guide him. Until he'd become brave. Until he'd become strong. Stronger than he'd ever imagined he could be.

But it had been too long since he'd tasted that strength. Eight months of fantasizing. Eight months of lying low, waiting for warm weather, waiting for the police and press to grow bored, waiting for word.

Now he was hungry to feel his power.

The glass door swung open and for a moment the rush of traffic outside eclipsed the low *thunk* of the bass guitar. The door closed and a dishwater blonde shouldering a duffel trudged past the vending machines and between rows of whirring washers.

He took a deep breath. The air smelled sweet with detergent and fabric softener. Not as sweet as her hair would smell. Not as sweet as the scent of her blood.

He'd never understand why women who would never walk down a dark street alone would brave a night like this to wash their laundry. Clean clothes were damn important to some people.

He smiled as she came closer.

She glanced at him with narrowed eyes.

He could see she was older than the ones he'd done last fall. Crow's feet touched the outer corners of her eyes. Her mouth held the pinched look of a woman who had to work hard to make ends meet. She was probably in her mid-thirties, maybe close to forty. He didn't like older women. They were warier, not as easily misled.

For a moment he considered walking out, checking a laundromat on the other side of town. The last thing he wanted was for her to figure him out and give his description to the police.

She opened one of the small top-loaders and sorted whites into it. Bras. Lacy panties.

He looked at her again, more closely this time. If her hair were a little lighter in color, if her lips were set in a cruel smile, she would look like his mother. Maybe he could even dress her in the slutty miniskirts his mother used to wear. And one of those oversize shirts with big shoulder pads that had gone out in the eighties.

He shifted in his chair. After eight long months, he'd fantasized enough. He wanted action.

Humming along with the radio, she plucked a small bottle of detergent from her duffel, measured it into the cap and poured it into the machine.

He stood up and crossed to one of the machines whose wash cycle had finished. Pulling out a few pairs of wet jeans, he mustered his most pitiful expression before throwing the clothes into a dryer near the woman. "Excuse me."

She glanced up at him, offering a stranger's smile, brief and insincere.

"My girlfriend says she doesn't like the smell of my clothes. She told me to get some of those dryer sheets. If you don't mind my asking, what kind do you use?"

She dipped a hand into her duffel and pulled out a pink box. "These smell the best and do a great job controlling static."

Got to be fast. Can't let her catch on. Not until I have her where I want her.

Reaching into his pocket, he tilted his head at the pink box, as if he really gave a damn about fabric softener. "Oh, I've seen commercials for that kind."

"Want to try one?"

"Sure. Thanks." He reached out as if he intended to take a sheet. Instead, he grabbed her arm.

Her eyes flew wide. She pulled back, trying to free herself, trying to fight.

He whipped his hand out of his pocket and stabbed the syringe into her arm. He held her as she fought.

Sleep. Fucking sleep, lady.

Finally she swayed and stumbled into him.

"Feels good, doesn't it? Feels real good." He'd never shot heroin himself, but that's what people said.

Moving quickly, before anyone else wandered into the laundromat, he pulled his laundry bag over her head. When he'd tugged it down past her waist, he positioned her swaying body next to a laundry cart and flopped her over. Lifting her by the hips, he heaved her into the cart.

A tinge of pain shot through his back. They were always heavier when they were deadweight. Once he let her loose in the forest, once she was fighting for her life, he wouldn't have to worry about back strain. Then the pain would all be hers.

He stuffed her feet into the oversized bag, pulled the drawstring closed, and tied it. Smiling to himself, he wheeled the cart to the exit and his waiting van.

Yes, laundromats were great for hunting. And he'd just bagged himself some prey.

Diana

Diana Gale had done everything she could think of to make her twin sister's post-wedding gift-opening a memory to cherish. She'd decorated her apartment with purple irises and white streamers. She'd poured mimosas and coffee for Sylvie's handful of out-of-town friends. And not much of a cook herself, she'd made brunch reservations at one of Madison's best restaurants. But as Sylvie sat on the couch next to her groom and tore open the card attached to the last silver-and-white package, Diana could tell something was wrong.

Clutching at the gift, Sylvie looked to her new groom. "Bryce."

"What is it?"

Sylvie spread the wedding card before Bryce Walker then looked up at Diana.

She didn't have to say who the gift was from. Diana knew by the alarm shining in her sister's blue eyes—eyes identical to hers.

Eyes identical to *his*.

A tremor crept up Diana's spine, raising the hair on the back of her neck. She hadn't spoken to their birth father in months, neither had Sylvie, but a day hadn't passed that they didn't both think about him. And Diana knew the door of communication she'd thrown open would never fully close.

"Who is it from?" One of Sylvie's friends who'd traveled up from Chicago for the wedding last night eyed Sylvie with a curious smile.

Diana plastered a smile to her own lips. Lisa might have been one of Sylvie's workmates from her previous life, but there was something about the woman that Diana didn't trust. It was as if she were constantly on the prowl for a wisp of gossip to provide herself with excitement, even at someone else's expense. The last thing either Sylvie or Diana needed was for any of these women to learn who had given this particular gift. "Just someone we know."

Sylvie leaned the gift against an end table and pushed to her feet. "You'll have to excuse me. I'm not feeling so well."

She darted from the room and down the hall toward Diana's bathroom. Bryce handed the card to Diana and started after his bride.

Serial killer Ed Dryden.

A father should have the privilege of walking his daughter down the aisle. I miss my girls. I look forward to your visit.

A newspaper clipping lay between the folds inside the card. Several months old, the newspaper article was dated October of the previous year.

Copycat Killer Claims Two

Diana hadn't expected Ed Dryden's silence to last forever. But this...

"Is Sylvie okay?" Lisa looked down the hall, eyes glowing with predatory interest.

"Maybe we should see if she needs anything," another friend offered.

"What's in that card?" asked a third.

Waving off their questions, Diana glanced at the gift, still shrouded in its silver-and-white wedding-bell paper, and then made a show of looking at her watch. "Why don't you guys head down to the restaurant?"

"The restaurant? Now?" Lisa shook her head. "I think we should help Sylvie."

"Bryce *is* helping her."

"There's only so much a man can do." Lisa stood up from her chair and plopped her hands on her hips. "I've been friends with Sylvie longer than any of you. I'll take care of it."

Diana tried to tamp down her annoyance. "Making sure the restaurant doesn't give away our table will be the most help, Lisa. Really."

Lisa frowned. Apparently she wanted more excitement than securing a spot for brunch would provide.

"Lisa, please." Diana offered her best pleading smile, praying the woman had the sense to stop pushing. "We'll be there before you know it."

"All right. But if the three of you don't join us soon, I'll be back to check on you." She gathered her posse and headed out of Diana's apartment.

As soon as the door shut behind them, Diana set the card on the counter and rushed to the bathroom door. "Sylvie?"

Bryce stepped out into the hall and closed the door behind him.

"How is she?"

"Sick. I'm sure all of us feel that way to some extent."

Diana couldn't agree more. But Diana's nausea was mixed with a heavy dose of guilt. "Is she going to be okay?"

Bryce paused, studying Diana's face. "We were going to wait to tell people, but you might as well know now."

"Know what?"

"Sylvie's pregnant."

"Oh, Bryce! That's wonderful. I know how much you both want a family. Congratulations."

"Thanks." Bryce smiled despite the concern still cloaking his brow. "But I'm worried about her. Especially with all this."

"You're leaving on your honeymoon tomorrow. She won't have to worry about it. At least not for a few weeks."

"If I can convince her to go."

"She has to go."

Bryce shrugged. "You know Sylvie. She's worried about you."

Her sister's concern would be touching if Diana weren't guilty of bringing this evil into Sylvie's life in the first place. "I'll be fine."

He gave a shallow nod, as if he wasn't so sure.

"Trust me. I can take care of myself this time. I will. You and Sylvie have a baby to think about."

He nodded, but again, his agreement wasn't convincing.

Diana knew he was remembering last October, when he and Sylvie had saved her after she'd been kidnapped from her own wedding. But that probably wasn't all. "You're thinking of your brother."

"I promised him… I promised myself that I'd find his killer. Dryden waving this Copycat Killer in our faces is a little hard to take."

Bryce believed the man who'd killed two women last fall was also responsible for his brother's death, a theory the police were still looking into, as far as she knew.

"You have to go through with the honeymoon, Bryce.

Sylvie needs you. And she doesn't need to be thinking about..."

Bryce held up a hand. "Believe me, my priorities are in order."

"What did the doctor say? You know, about her heart condition?" As a child, Sylvie had suffered from heart problems, the reason she had been left behind in the foster care system while Diana had been adopted. In the year since they'd been reunited, Sylvie hadn't had any health problems, but that didn't mean the extra stress of dealing with Ed Dryden piled on top of her pregnancy wasn't a recipe for disaster.

"He said she should avoid extra stress. And I aim to make sure she takes that advice."

The bathroom door opened and Sylvie stepped out into the hall. Her cheeks looked flushed, her eyes a bit glassy. "If the two of you are done deciding my future, why don't we see what's in that package?"

Bryce cupped her elbow gently in one hand and searched her face. "Are you sure you're up to it?"

"I'm pretty sure I'm *not* up to it. But that doesn't mean I'm not going to see what he sent. I'm sure my heart can take that much."

"I didn't mean anything by that," Diana said. God knew that of the two of them, Sylvie was the strong one. Diana had only to think back to that cabin in the woods for proof.

"I know. You're just watching out for me. What families do, right?" Sylvie offered a smile. "I'm still getting used to that."

"Yeah. What families do." Diana took a deep breath, trying to quell the flutter in her chest and stomach. After all she'd been through in that cabin last fall, Diana had sworn she would become more like her sister. Strong. Independent.

And eight months later, she finally felt as if she was making some progress.

If Sylvie was willing to face Dryden's gift, so was Diana. "Okay. Let's open the thing."

The three of them returned to the living room. Bryce and Sylvie took their places on the couch.

Diana propped a hip on the couch's arm.

Grabbing the gift from where she'd left it, Sylvie took a deep breath, and then tore a corner of the paper free and slid out a simple black frame holding a family portrait.

A father, a mother, and two little girls around three years old smiled for the camera. Soft blond hair curled around the children's identical features. One of them cradled a clown puppet. The other tangled her fingers together in her lap, her face chalky and frail looking. The mother held her blond head high, her lips pressed into a commanding smile. The father stood behind the three, staring directly into the camera with ice-blue eyes.

"It's us," whispered Sylvie. "My God, it's us."

Diana stared at the portrait, a mixture of heat and nerves descending into her chest. "I'm so sorry, Sylvie."

"For what?"

"For bringing him into your life." She rubbed her forehead. "What was I thinking? When I found out he was my biological father, why couldn't I have just left well enough alone? Why did I have to see him?"

"Because you needed to know where you came from. You needed to understand who you were."

"Which is what?" *The daughter of a serial killer?* Her mind shuddered at the thought.

"Which is my sister." Sylvie touched her hand to Diana's arm, her trembling fingers belying the steadiness in her voice.

"Sometimes we just need to know. No matter what the consequences. I would have done the same thing, Diana. You know that."

She did. But that didn't make her feel any less responsible. "I have to stop him."

Bryce looked from one sister to the other. "What are you going to do?"

"I don't know yet. But I know who might." Although eight months had passed since Diana had given back his ring, sometimes it felt like yesterday. "I'm going to take the portrait and card to Bobby."

Sylvie thrust to her feet. "I'll go with you."

Diana held out a palm as if that would hold Sylvie in place. "You have a baby to worry about."

"I'm pregnant, not crippled."

"No, but you're sick."

She gave a shrug, as if morning sickness was nothing. But the pale sheen to her skin told the real story.

"Besides, you still have guests to deal with. The last thing we need is to have Lisa storming back demanding answers."

Sylvie opened her mouth to protest, but Bryce cut her off. "We'll take care of Lisa. Tell Bobby to call me."

"Of course."

Sylvie pressed her lips together. "We're in this together, Diana. Remember that."

Diana nodded. They *were* in this together. Whether Sylvie deserved to be or not. And now it was Diana's turn to contribute, to be strong for once... to bring what she'd started to an end.

FRANTIC
ORDER NOW!

A VICTIM'S VOW

A killer kidnapped her... from her own wedding. Barely escaping, Diana Gale vowed to never be a victim again. That's when the copycat came calling. Now Diana has no choice to put her life—and her trust—in hands of the fiancé she'd left months before.

A COP'S DEVOTION

Detective Bobby Vaughan still loves Diana. But can he forgive her for leaving him? When his job demands he protect the woman who crushed his heart, he'll have to put love and forgiveness to the test.

A PREDATOR'S OBSESSION

All artists have muses. If your art is murder, you are

inspired by the master who came before you, and the apprentice who follows...

A SERIAL KILLER'S DAUGHTER.
A cop trying to protect his own.
A dark evil pulling the strings.

FRANTIC by Ann Voss Peterson
There's no place to hide...

SMALL TOWN SECRETS: SINS
-LETHAL
-CAPTIVE
-FRANTIC
-VICIOUS
Read them all!

BOOKS BY ANN VOSS PETERSON:

VAL RYKER THRILLERS

Pushed Too Far

Burned Too Hot

Dead Too Soon

Watched Too Long (with J.A. Konrath)

Buried Too Deep (release date TBA)

SMALL TOWN SECRETS

The smallest towns have the most to hide...

Small Town Secrets: Sins

Lethal

Captive

Frantic

Vicious

Small Town Secrets: Scandals

Witness

Stolen

Malice

Guilty

Forbidden

Kidnapped

Small Town Secrets: Short Stories

The School

CODENAME: CHANDLER, by Ann Voss Peterson and J.A. Konrath

Hit

Exposed

Fix (with F. Paul Wilson)

Naughty

Flee

Spree

Three

Rescue

ROCKY MOUNTAIN THRILLERS

Manhunt

Fugitive

Justice

Maverick

Renegade

Short Stories:

Babe On Board (with J.A. Konrath)

Wild Night Is Calling (with J.A. Konrath)

PARANORMAL ROMANTIC SUSPENSE

GYPSY MAGIC
Part 1: Wyatt (Justice is Blind)

Part 2: Garner (Love is Death)

Part 3: Andrei (The Law is Impotent)

RENEGADE MAGIC
Part 1: Luke by Rebecca York

Part 2: Tom by Ann Voss Peterson

Part 3: Rico by Patricia Rosemoor

NEW ORLEANS MAGIC
Part 1: Jordan by Rebecca York

Part 2: Liam by Ann Voss Peterson

Part 3: Zachary by Patricia Rosemoor

RETURN TO JENKINS COVE
Book 1: Christmas Spirit by Rebecca York

Book 2: Christmas Awakening by Ann Voss Peterson

Book 3: Christmas Delivery by Patricia Rosemoor

SECURITY BREACH
Book 1: Chain Reaction by Rebecca York

Book 2: Critical Exposure by Ann Voss Peterson

Book 3: Triggered Response by Patricia Rosemoor

OTHER ROMANTIC SUSPENSE
Laying Down the Law (Chicago Confidential series), Harlequin Intrigue

Legally Binding (Shotgun Sallys series), Harlequin Intrigue

Special Assignment (Bodyguards Unlimited series), Harlequin Intrigue

Seized by the Sheik (Cowboys Royale series), Harlequin Intrigue

Secret Protector (Situation: Christmas series), Harlequin Intrigue

Books by **MELINDA DUCHAMP**

(comic erotica co-written by Peterson & Konrath)

MAKE ME BLUSH Series

#1-Mister Kink

#2-Fifty Shades of Witch

ALICE Series

#1-Fifty Shades Of Alice In Wonderland

#2-Fifty Shades Of Alice Through The Looking Glass

#3-Fifty Shades Of Alice At The Hellfire Club

JEZEBEL Series

#1-Fifty Shades Of Jezebel And The Beanstalk

#2-Fifty Shades Of Puss In Boots

#3-Fifty Shades Of Goldilocks

SEXPERTS Series

#1-The Sexperts - Fifty Grades Of Shay

#2-The Sexperts - The Girl With The Pearl Necklace

#3-The Sexperts - Loving the Alien

ABOUT THE AUTHOR

ANN VOSS PETERSON is the author of over thirty novels and has millions of books in print all over the globe. Winner of the prestigious Daphne du Maurier Award and a Rita finalist, Ann is known for her adrenaline-fueled thrillers and romantic suspense novels, including the Codename: Chandler spy thrillers she writes with J.A. Konrath and her own thriller series featuring small town Wisconsin police chief Val Ryker.

A creative writing major in college, Ann worked all manner of jobs after graduation, ranging from grooming show horses to washing windows, and now she draws on her wide variety of life experiences to fill her fictional worlds with compelling energy and undeniable emotion.

She lives near Madison, Wisconsin with her family and their border collie.

Visit Ann at www.AnnVossPeterson.com, and check out the behind-the-scenes research that goes into her books.

To find out about each new Ann Voss Peterson story as they are released and get a free book sign up for her newsletter on her website.

Copyright Notice

Captive

Portions of this novel were previously published under the title Serial Bride.

Copyright © 2006, 2020 by Ann Voss Peterson

Cover and art copyright © 2016 by Carl Graves

This book is a work of fiction. Names, characters, places and incidents are either products of the author's imagination or used fictitiously. Any resemblance to actual events, locales, or persons, living or dead, is entirely coincidental. All rights reserved. No part of this publication can be reproduced or transmitted in any form or by any means, electronic or mechanical, without permission in writing from the author.

January, 2020

❦ Created with Vellum

Made in the USA
Coppell, TX
10 May 2021